RESCUED

CATHERINE ALBA

LAURA

THE CAB DROPPED me off outside the beach house. As it drove away back up the street, I turned slowly and took in the view. It was a beautiful place, right on the beach, and some gardener that my parents probably under-paid had done a great job out front. Keeping up appearances with the HOA, I guessed, since my parents were hardly ever here to enjoy the scent from the heavy rose bushes themselves. Right now, they were on a cruise somewhere off the coast of the Bahamas. Or was it Barbados?

Never mind. I would have the house to myself for most of the summer; that was the point. Glorious sun, sand, and solitude. Exactly what I needed. Rest, recuperation, and plenty of time to think. It would have been heaven if it hadn't been for the memories of last summer that had started to crowd up on me as soon as I stepped out of the taxi.

I determinedly pushed those memories to the back of my mind and focused on what I'd been telling myself. A year was a long time. So much could happen in a year. People moved. Got new jobs in faraway places. Got run over by drunk drivers. Flattened by frozen poo from a passing airplane.

The only way I'd been able to return here had been the conviction that everyone had moved on. In a place like this, people came and went. It was a holiday paradise, and no one spent their entire life on holiday.

No one from that night would still be around. Surely?

As if on cue, a beach buggy came roaring up the sandy beach toward me. The grating engine sound made me snatch up my two bags and hurry up the steps to the front porch. Tapping in the six-digit code into the lock with trembling fingers, I could feel the hairs on the back of my neck standing up.

Please, please, please let me just get through the door before they saw me.

Because despite my convictions, I just knew it had to be him.

No one else would careen up the beach making such a racket, with no consideration for anyone else.

Fucking Jonas.

No, that had been the problem, hadn't it? That I hadn't wanted to fuck him. Not on his terms.

The digital lock finally accepted the numbers my trembling fingers had pressed, and the door opened with a click. Dragging one of my bags and kicking the other across the threshold, I hurried inside and pulled the door closed behind me. My heart was racing in my chest as I leaned over to look out the small peephole.

The buggy bounced over the nearest dune and came to a halt behind the fence across the road from the house next door. Oh, it was him all right. I would have known that blond piece of shit anywhere.

How was it possible? He had graduated last year, and he'd been going on and on about how that summer was his last on the beach. How he'd have to get a real job and never wear shorts for work again.

I had been so sure that he wouldn't be here, but here he was. Right next door. What a nightmare!

He jumped out of the buggy and strode across the road, his long fringe obscuring his face until he had almost reached the porch. Just before he disappeared out of sight, he turned his head in my direction, looking back over his shoulder.

Fucking Jonas. Still as handsome as ever. But his dashing blond looks didn't cause my body to tingle in the same way as it had done at the start of last summer. On the contrary, it gave me the creeps.

And I was starting to think that no boy would ever make me tingle in that particular way, ever again. He had ruined sex for me. Ruined my body, perhaps for life.

Shivering, I picked up my bags and started to make my way through the house. It was light outside, but most of the shutters were closed, so the rooms were cloaked in semi-darkness. I wasn't about to open the shutters because I didn't want to signal to the neighborhood—and particularly not to one of the residents next door—that I was here, so I'd just have to get used to it. I didn't have a choice.

I'd begged my mother to let me stay at their house back home in Seattle, but she was having the entire house redecorated while they were away on their cruise, and the house wouldn't be habitable until August at the earliest. I was on the waiting list for half a dozen apartments back home, but I knew I wouldn't get a lease if I didn't get a job first. And getting a job in Seattle was going to be difficult if I was living in a beach house in Florida. I had tried to explain this to my mother, but she had refused to listen.

"You should have thought of that," she had said, her voice as condescending as always. "You should have gotten a job. It's not as if graduation came as a surprise. You knew that you'd have to move out of the dorm."

My mother was the most infuriating woman on the planet. Of course, I'd known. It was just that I'd assumed that I could stay at their house while I figured some stuff out. Their McMansion was always empty over the summer, since my parents liked to travel, so I thought I'd save some money and just camp out there.

I'd never dreamed that my own parents would leave me stranded like this.

OK, so I should have found a job. But that wasn't as easy as it sounded in this economy, and besides, I didn't have a clue as to what I wanted to do, or even where in the world I wanted to do it. It seemed as if every choice I might make eliminated so many different options, and I wasn't prepared to close any doors. Not at 21 years of age. Surely that was too soon to settle? And I honestly hadn't believed that I'd have to, since my parents were pretty well off. I had thought that they'd want to take care of me until I had figured out what I wanted to do with my life.

Some people—close personal friends of mine, for instance—might think that I was a bit ungrateful. After all, my parents had let me stay in their fancy beach house right on the sand in Florida for the summer, rent-free. That was a pretty sweet deal. And normally, I would agree. But this particular beach house was the last place I wanted to be. Not that it was a bad house. And it certainly wasn't a bad beach. Lexington was the best beach on the whole Florida coastline, no doubt about it. It was just …

That fucking Jonas.

I'd had a crush on the boy next door last summer, and it had ended badly. I had left here in tears, swearing that I'd never come back, hoping that the whole town would be wiped out in some freakish tropical storm.

It hadn't been.

And now, here I was.

I dropped my bags in the living room and walked over to the patio doors. After spending a minute or so figuring out how the lock worked, I slid one of them open. The back garden was as well-tended as the front, which was a good thing because it seemed I would be spending all my time there. I certainly didn't intend to set foot on the beach, where Jonas and his buddies ruled. Fucking lifeguards.

Just a year ago, that had been my goal, literally. But this summer …? The best I could hope for was a nice all-over tan. The garden was secluded enough that I wouldn't have to worry about tan lines.

I left the patio door open and went to get changed out of my clothes.

2

PELLE

I HAD BEEN in the middle of a fascinating book on the history of the Silk Road when Jonas came back from his morning shift as a lifeguard. I could hear him coming from a mile away, and when the front door slammed, I put the book down with a sigh. Hurricane Jonas was in the house. My tranquility was shattered for the foreseeable future.

Sure enough, music started blaring from the built-in speakers all over the house. I cursed and reached for my phone, switching off all the speakers apart from those in the kitchen, where I could hear Jonas plundering the fridge.

I think it was about time that my son moved out. I had expected him to want to, but the reality was that he'd have to get a job if he wanted his own apartment, and that would mean cutting back on his hours on the beach. Perhaps quitting the lifeguards all together. And Jonas hadn't been prepared to give up his cushy summer job. It paid peanuts but came with amazing fringe benefits, most of them wearing thong bikinis.

We'd had a terrible row about the mess he made and how he treated this place like a hotel, of course, and I'd even gone so far as to call his mother to discuss the situation.

That had been a bad idea.

"You barely spent any time with the boy during his entire childhood, and now when you've finally built up some kind of relationship, you want to throw him out onto the street?" Lana had said, her voice about as seductive as a bag full of poisoned razorblades.

"I never said anything about throwing him out," I'd protested. "I just thought he might be expected to … you know… stand on his own two feet at the age of 22."

She'd snorted. "Like you were some serious professional at his age? Perhaps he just takes after his deadbeat dad?"

I didn't bother replying. I certainly didn't mention the fact that this deadbeat dad had supported his son and that son's bitch of a mother for the last fifteen years, keeping them in an opulent lifestyle that they all too easily had become accustomed to, and none of them seemed to want to stand on their own two feet as long as they could get me to foot their bills.

Hearing the fruit of my loins thunder through the ground floor of my beach house, I considered if it wouldn't be worth it to just buy Jonas a place of his own. An apartment somewhere close to his beloved beach. Give him an allowance but make it clear that it was for the summer only. Come autumn, he would have to get a job and support himself. I just couldn't have him around. We weren't close, and I didn't feel any particular bond to the boy. I felt responsible, that was all.

And that wasn't enough to build a family on.

Stretching to relieve the tension that always built in my neck when I thought of my son, I glanced out the window. It looked like a nice day. Perhaps I should go for a run before it got too hot. And by the time I got back, Jonas would have gone to sleep. He always took an afternoon nap so that he could stay up late and party with his friends and still make the morning shift at the lifeguard station.

I got up and walked over to the window. It might already be too hot for a run. The sun seemed to be pelting down.

A movement in the garden next door caught my eye. That was weird. Their gardener always came on Tuesdays. I'd heard their weed whacker yesterday; I was sure of that. No one was supposed to be over there today. The Johnson's were on a cruise in the West Indies and wouldn't be back until August.

But there was definitely someone there. I couldn't quite see them from this window, though.

With a worried frown, I made my way along the upstairs hallway to my office at the back of the house. That was the only room that had an unhindered view of next door's garden. If there were burglars in the neighborhood and I didn't do anything, it might be my house that got broken into next. I had to check it out. It was the responsible and neighborly thing to do.

Everyone thought it was madness having my office back here when I had so many rooms with a beach view, but I knew myself, and that beautiful scenery would only distract me. I needed the dark paneled walls and heavy curtains to shut out the summer-all-year-round paradise outside the windows. Compared to where I came from, this place was paradise, and if I were to get any real work done, I had to pretend that I was somewhere else. Somewhere where there were actual seasons. Where it rained or even snowed.

Entering my office, I hurried across to the window, pulling my phone out of my pocket, ready to record any intruders with my high-def camera for the police. It could be used as evidence. Perhaps I wouldn't even need to testify.

But as I stared out the window, my phone held up to the glass to avoid lens glare, any

thoughts of burglars and home security vanished from my mind.

That was no burglar. At least not like any burglar I had ever seen.

It was a girl. A young girl. And she was sunbathing. In the nude.

The sun lounger she lay on was pulled out to the edge of the back patio, and she had not opened the parasol that usually shielded the matching loungers from the scorching mid-day sun. She was lying on her stomach, her head resting on her arms, and I could see the bright red cord of her headphones snaking from her ear to the phone that rested on the striped white-and-navy fabric of the lounger next to her head.

Her round butt cheeks were completely bare, and it was obvious that she normally wore bikini bottoms and a top. The white stripe across her back and the pale triangle across her curvy bottom glared at me, looking almost lit-up from where I was standing. I couldn't take my eyes off her.

Not until she moved did I notice that I was still standing there, my phone raised. I knew it was wrong but couldn't make myself stop the recording as she slowly turned over on her back, giving me a glorious view of a pair of magnificent breasts. Her eyes were closed, and one of her legs were pulled up slightly. Even though I was quite far away, I could see that she had waxed almost all her pubic hair, leaving only a narrow strip of hair.

She was a natural blond.

It slowly dawned on me that this must be the Johnsons' daughter. I had only met her briefly last summer. She and Jonas had been an item for all of five minutes, but nothing had come of it, as far as I knew. That realization made me finally switch off the recording and shove the phone back in my pocket. Thank goodness that she hadn't seen me up here, gawking at her like some old pervert. She probably didn't even realize that anyone could see her down there. All the back gardens on this street were very secluded.

I allowed myself another few seconds of admiring that magnificent young body but then forced myself to move away from the window, feeling like a dirty old man. She was half my age, for crying out loud. Perhaps she and Jonas would make another go of it this summer. But regardless of what happened between them, it would be madly inappropriate of me to peep at her like that when she wasn't aware of me looking.

Madly inappropriate.

And insanely arousing.

3

LAURA

I HAD SLEPT WELL, even though I'd managed to get a slight sunburn on my first day—on the parts that weren't used to complete exposure—and awoke early the next morning. Rolling over in bed, I looked over at the thick curtains that covered my bedroom windows. There was a glow around the edges that told me that the sun was up.

Dragging myself out of bed, I pulled on some yoga pants and a T-shirt and toddled off to the bathroom for some morning ablutions. When I got back and grabbed a hoodie and my phone, I was stunned to see the time. A quarter to six! I hadn't been up this early since … I couldn't even remember.

But it was a good thing that I was, because I needed to go on a grocery run, and this was the best time to do it if I wanted to make sure that I didn't run into anyone I knew. Or who knew me. Knew *of* me. There were probably plenty of those around here.

The fridge was empty, but I slipped a coffee pod into the maker and waited while the black fluid seeped down into my to-go-mug. As soon as the machine went quiet, I grabbed it and headed for the door.

The street was almost completely deserted, apart from the occasional dog walker and jogger, that all seemed to be either on their way to the beach or coming back from there. I walked toward the shop a couple of blocks down, sipping my coffee. It was surprisingly chilly out, and I was glad that I had thought to bring a sweater. Pulling the sleeves down over my hands, I shuddered and took another sip. The coffee was strong but not particularly good. My parents may be snobs in many ways, but they were surprisingly ignorant when it came to coffee.

With a pang, I thought about Felicity and Heather and our summers at The Grind, all the different variations we had come up with during lulls in our shifts, some of which had turned out to be pretty darn good. I had actually gotten relatively skilled at making coffee, if I did say so myself, and I would have to pick up some proper beans while I was at the store.

The store had just opened when I arrived, and I was one of the first people there. The isles were mostly deserted, and I walked back and forth, trying to decide on a menu for my stay here. What was the best plan for getting through this summer? I would need to stay sane despite my isolation and also have the energy and clarity needed to do some serious thinking and planning. I had the rest of my life to figure out, and that didn't happen in one afternoon.

So, should I go with comfort foods that would keep me calm and take the edge of the stress that would inevitably follow my decision struggles? Just forget about what that might do to my weight loss goals and focus on sugars and carbs? That would certainly ease the boredom and loneliness like nothing else. Or should I make this the summer when

I broke my upwards trajectory and learned to love healthy snacks?

Yeah, I don't think so.

It was bad enough that I was stuck here all alone for the summer. If I couldn't even have my good friends Ben and Jerry to keep me company, I'd soon go straight out of my mind.

And that was a dangerous thing to do in a place where people didn't necessarily have my back. I would need to keep my head on straight, or I might have to leave Florida in tears once again. And then where would I go?

I also had to watch my spending, and in the end, I forced myself to return a few non-essential items. How I was going to feed myself all summer, I had no idea. I knew that dad would send me some money as long as mom wasn't around when I asked him, but I hated having to do that. I was a grown woman, albeit unemployed, and I needed to find a way to support myself.

Perhaps I could get a job somewhere around here?

I paid for my groceries, smarting a bit

when I saw the red digits on the small screen. It would be fine, I told myself; I could make it work.

But as I walked back the same way I'd come, I couldn't help but wonder if perhaps I couldn't. And then what?

I had never been any kind of over-achiever, even though I was quite capable when I had a clear goal. The problem was that I didn't have a life goal, clear or other-wise, apart from 'have a fulfilling career' or even 'be happy.' And the problem with those goals was that they were too vague. There was no Step 1, no clear path from where I was to where I wanted to go. Right now, I couldn't even see how I could get from where I was to anywhere I wanted to be, and that was depressing.

I just knew that I didn't want to be *here*, where I was now.

In fact, I'd rather be anywhere but here.

As I approached the beach house, I felt myself growing tense, and my eyes darted back and forth between the sidewalk ahead and the beach on the other side of the street. It was way too early for lifeguards to be out on the beach, but what if Jonas had a dentist's appointment or an errand to run? There could be a million reasons why he'd decide to leave the house at the crack of dawn. If not today, then at some other time when I had ventured outside.

It was stupid to think that I would be able to stay in the house next door to where he was living all summer and not run into him, but I just couldn't imagine how I would cope with it if I did.

I just couldn't face him.

So, when I heard a front door open, just as I approached the gate to my parents' house, I felt my heart racing in my chest. Was it the door to Jonas's house, or could it have been somewhere further down the street? I didn't dare to look, just hurried toward the gate, hoping, praying even. Please, let it be someone else. Anyone else.

Fast footsteps came toward me, and I turned my face toward the house, trying to hide inside the hood of my sweatshirt. Jonas didn't know that I was here, so he might not realize that it was me. As long as he didn't see my face.

Oh, please, *please* let it not be him.

I felt more than saw the tall, imposing shape come toward me. He was jogging at a quick pace, almost running, and I panicked. The gate was still a few feet ahead of me, and there was nowhere to go. The sidewalk was too narrow and the fence too tall for me to climb. I walked closer to it, feeling the sleeve of my hoodie brushing against the planks. As the man came past me, I pressed myself against the wood. I may or may not have whimpered out loud. Pathetic, I know, but I was not feeling brave right at this moment.

Please, please, just go away. Just keep running. Please, don't look at me!

But the quick steps slowed and then stopped. Even though I had my back toward the man, I could sense him turning toward me. Coming closer. I was in full panic mode now and could barely breathe. The gate! It was just there. I could make it if I just—

"Laura?"

Hearing my name spoken right behind my back was the final straw. I bolted, dropping my bag of groceries to the ground and speeding toward the garden gate.

"Laura!" said the man behind me as I tore open the gate, flung myself inside, and slammed it shut behind me, racing up the path toward the veranda. "It's only me! I'm so sorry; I didn't mean to scare you. It's me. Jonas's dad."

I was so frantic; it took forever for the words to sink in. I was already up the front stairs, blindly pressing the buttons to the digital lock. The red light came on—wrong code—and I just stared at it. What was the code again?

My mind went completely blank. I couldn't for the life of me remember. Six digits. I had known the code yesterday, but now …

"Laura?" said the voice again. It sounded genuinely concerned.

Slowly I turned toward it. It wasn't Jonas. I could see that. But the man who was standing right outside the gate bore a striking resemblance to the boy who had ruined my life last summer. Just as tall. At least just as handsome. He was also wearing a hoodie, and when he pushed the hood down to reveal his face, his hair was just as impossibly blond as the gorgeous lifeguard who lived next door. The eyes that regarded me with concern were just as blue.

But where Jonas's eyes had been arrogant and cocky, brimming with self-importance and confidence, these eyes were worried and empathetic. Caring, even. The contrast from what I had been expecting was jarring and unsettling.

"M-mr Lindstrom?" I said, my voice fractured and frail. The fear vanished immediately but was replaced by shame and embarrassment. Both over my foolish behavior just now, but also because of what had happened last summer. Surely, Mr. Lindstrom must have heard. Perhaps he had even seen the footage. I felt dirty, just thinking about it.

"I didn't mean to scare you," he said.

I shook my head. "I— you didn't. I thought you were someone else," I mumbled. I couldn't very well tell him that I had thought that he was his son, and that I feared meeting that boy more than anything right now.

"You dropped your bag," he said, moving

up the street a bit and then coming back, holding the shopping bag over the fence toward me.

I pulled myself together and walked down the steps. The bag had torn a little on one side, and something red was seeping slowly out through the rift. It looked like blood, and it took a moment before I realized that it must be the tomato juice I had bought. It had come in a glass bottle. I didn't want to think about what the red liquid and the glass shards would have done to the rest of my food.

"Thank you," I mumbled, taking the bag from his hand. He didn't let go. I forced myself to look him in the eye and was shocked by the intensity with which he was regarding me.

"Are you all right, Laura?" he asked, and his voice was so sincere, as if he actually cared. "I certainly didn't mean to scare you. I wasn't thinking. There aren't usually that many people out at this time of day, so I wasn't paying any attention to my surroundings. I am so sorry." He looked at the red puddle by my feet. "Your groceries are bleeding."

I nodded. "It's nothing. Just some juice." I tugged at the bag again, but he still didn't want to let go.

"Let me replace that for you," he said. "And anything else that might have been ruined." He glanced up at the house behind me. "Your parents aren't around, are they?" I shook my head. "On a cruise, right?" I nodded. "Are you staying here all alone?"

I hesitated but then nodded again. "Thanks, but I'm sure the rest of the food is fine." A more determined tug, and I finally managed to pull the bag from his hand. "My parents won't be back until August. It's nice to have the place to myself." I forced a smile and avoided meeting his bright blue eyes.

It felt almost disturbing to see Jonas's eyes look back at me with such concern. In reality, the look in his eyes had been the complete opposite. Scorn. Disgust. And something that reminded me of how a predator might look at its prey, right before tearing it to shreds.

"I have to go," I mumbled and hurried away.

"If you need anything," he called after me, "Jonas and I are right next door."

I could feel ice-cold chills running down my spine and forced myself to turn around and look at Mr. Lindstrom. "If you don't mind," I said, hoping that my voice didn't sound as frail to him as it did in my own ears, "I'd appreciate it if you didn't tell Jonas that I am here."

He looked surprised, his light, almost golden eyebrows moving quite a way up toward the thick blond hair. "All right," he said slowly. "Mind if I ask why?"

I could feel tears welling up and used up the last of my willpower to keep them back, just for a moment longer. "I'd just really prefer it," I said, "if he didn't know that I am here."

It was impossible to keep the tears back any longer. So many intense emotions that had been pent up for too long burst through the dam I had built up over the last year to contain them all. I quickly turned and hurried back up the stairs to the front porch. By some miracle, I managed to remember the code to the front door, and I slipped inside, pulling the door closed behind me, not relaxing until I heard the lock go click.

Trembling with sobs, I turned and peeped outside. Mr. Lindstrom stood by the gate, one arm resting on the top of it, looking straight at me. I knew he couldn't see me, but it still felt strange. Would he do it? Would he keep my secret? Or would he go straight back home and ask his son why the girl next door started crying when he had mentioned his name?

I didn't even want to think about what would happen if he did that.

But I couldn't think of anything else.

This summer was going to be hell.

4

PELLE

I HAD OBVIOUSLY FRIGHTENED the poor girl, and it felt awful, but what was I going to do about it? Following her up the stairs and banging on her front door wasn't going to reassure her, even though that was my intention. The more I had tried to apologize, the more upset she had seemed.

That poor girl.

She was even more beautiful up close than I remembered from last summer. The girl that Jonas had brought home with him a couple of times had been bright and bouncy, always with a wide smile on her face. This year's Laura had been downcast. Demure, almost. Sad, definitely. I had seen the tears well up in her eyes, even though she had tried to hide it when she hurried away.

Hurried away from me, the man who had scared her out of her wits.

I felt like a monster, and that was no pleasant feeling. I picked up the pace, glancing up and down the street before crossing to the other side and running down the path to the beach. It had been a while since I'd been out running, but yesterday's restlessness had driven me out of bed at the crack of dawn, and I'd known that I needed some intense physical exertion if I was to be able to focus on work later.

The sand right at the water's edge was packed and dark from the retreating waves, perfectly smooth and wide open, no one else around. I ran faster than I normally would, pushing myself harder, maybe just to snap out of the funk from the last few days or perhaps as a punishment for my behavior this morning.

Scaring a young girl like that.

It couldn't be easy living alone in that big house all summer. Why hadn't she brought a friend or a boyfriend to keep her company? I was sure that there would be plenty of young men who would love to spend the summer with her, even in less flashy surroundings. She was gorgeous, to say the least, and those curves …

Oh, dear.

I picked up the pace another notch and felt my chest starting to ache from the strain. Serves you right, you dirty old man, I told myself. Lusting after a girl like that, you should be ashamed of yourself.

And I was. Truly.

But that didn't stop me from reliving those glorious moments yesterday when I'd stood in my office, staring down at her naked body on the patio next door, basking in the sun, radiant with youth and beauty.

I must have stepped in a dent in the sand or something because suddenly my right foot bent underneath me, and I fell, tumbling ass over head straight into the hard, packed sand.

During a second or two, I didn't know which way was up but then my muscle memories from when I used to take judo lessons kicked in, and I tucked my head in and rolled, just in time. I landed on my back, but not as completely winded as I might have been, and as I lay there staring up at the clear blue sky, it didn't seem as if anything was broken. My heart was racing in a way that was almost painful, and my muscles were tingly from the exertion, but the only thing that really hurt was my right ankle.

Gingerly, I got up and tried to walk. My ankle said no, in no uncertain terms. Cursing under my breath, I turned and hobbled back in the direction I had come. I was surprised to see how far I had run. It felt as if I had just set out.

It took forever to hobble the distance that I had covered in only a few minutes running, and by the time I approached the house, my right foot was throbbing and felt swollen. Damn it.

As I struggled past the Johnsons' house, I couldn't help but look up. The guilt from this morning was even overshadowing the pain I was in. I noticed that the shutters were closed and thought that I might offer to help her remove them later, but then I realized that I wouldn't be climbing any ladders for a while. Perhaps I could ask Jonas to do it?

But no. Laura didn't want Jonas to know that she was here.

That was strange. I wondered why she would feel the need to hide her presence here from him. As I recalled, they had been good friends, at least for a while. She had left rather abruptly, but Jonas hadn't mentioned anything about a fight or anything. I didn't think that they had been a serious couple, but I had thought at the time that she'd seemed to have a crush on my son.

Knowing Jonas, he had probably broken her heart by going off with some other girl right in front of her nose. He was a short-sighted bastard, and as much as I hated to admit it, he probably got it from me. At least when I was younger, I hadn't always been the perfect gentleman.

I'd like to think that things would be different now, but it had been a long time since I'd met a woman that I'd felt any urge at all to pursue a relationship with.

Pushing open my garden gate, I realized that the only woman who had made my blood boil in a long time was the girl next door. Honestly, how desperate would a man need to be before he tried to seduce a girl half his age?

Honestly, how desperate was I?

I shook my head, trying to rid myself of the unsettling emotions, and the memories of her luscious naked breasts and that narrow strip of hair that disappeared down between her legs. Limping up the stairs, I groaned out loud, and it was only partly because of the pain from my ankle. Part of it was the intense lust that had stirred inside of me. Pathetic, truly.

She probably already had a boyfriend. Of course, she did. A beautiful girl like that? She probably had boyfriends lining up around the block. She would never look twice at an old dude like me.

I hobbled inside and made my way into the kitchen. It was still as tidy as I had left it, which meant that Jonas wasn't up yet. He had come home late last night. Again. He'd said something about a date, and at the time, I hadn't thought much about it, but as I limped over to the freezer to get an icepack for my ankle, I thought that perhaps I needed to do something about getting a date, myself.

I had to be jonesing for it if I was lusting after the neighbors' daughter!

I grabbed a water bottle from the fridge and sat down at the kitchen island, my swollen foot on the barstool next to mine, icepack balanced on top of my ankle. After a couple of swigs, I tried to remove my running shoe. Usually, I just kicked them off, but this morning it took me almost five minutes to gingerly loosen the shoe and pry it off my swollen foot. Removing the sock, I grimaced. This did not look good. I might need an x-ray.

I heard footsteps coming down the hall, and when I looked up, Jonas ambled into view. He grunted something inarticulate.

"Good morning," I said, trying to keep the acid I felt from my voice.

Another grunt.

"I might need you to take me to the emergency room," I said.

He had reached for the fridge door handle but stopped with his hand midair. "What? Why?"

I nodded at my propped-up foot, ice pack on top.

"Oh," he said, but he didn't seem overly concerned. "I have to go to work."

I frowned. "When?"

"I start at nine."

I glanced at the clock on the wall. "Drive me now, then," I said. "There's plenty of time. I can get a taxi back if you don't have time to wait for me."

He grimaced. "Then why can't you just take a taxi there, as well?"

I felt the annoyance that tinted every conversation I had with my son start to rise. "Because I have my grown-up son living *rent-free* with me at the moment, and he doesn't start work for another two hours, so he has plenty of time to drive me in the car *that I leased for him.*"

I didn't even bother hiding the acid.

Jonas shrugged. I felt like shaking him. Had I been that obnoxious when I was a kid? I didn't think so.

"I'm going to take a shower," I said, restraining the urge to shout at him. "When I get back, I want you to drive me to the ER."

He glowered at me but grunted something that I took to be an affirmative answer. Cursing under my breath, I made my way upstairs to my bathroom. I hadn't been running for long but was covered in sweat and sand, and it felt great to crank up all the nozzles until I was pelted from all directions with hot water. The water pressure here was great, much better than my apartment in New York. I grabbed a handful of soap and lathered my body, washing my hair and rinsing it until I couldn't feel any more grains of sand in my scalp. Running one hand down to wash my privates, my thoughts turned to yesterday's surprise revelation next door, and thinking about her naked butt cheeks with the pale triangle made me go rock hard. A soapy fist relieved the tension while I rested my forehead against the cold tiles and thought about what it would feel like to shove my hard shaft in between those smooth and soft peachy mounds.

It was a horrible thing to be lusting after such a young and innocent girl. But as long as she never knew what I did when I thought about her, I guess there was no harm done.

And she would never know what I had seen that day.

HALF AN HOUR LATER, I had gotten shaved and dressed and limped outside to the Prius that I had leased for Jonas this summer. I thought about getting in the back seat but instead opted for the passenger seat. If I pushed the seat as far back as it would go, it would be fine, but I lifted my swollen foot into the footwell with both hands, careful not to bang my leg against anything. The pain was even more intense now.

Jonas didn't speak, but his face communicated volumes as he sighed and frowned and grimaced at every turn between my house and the hospital's emergency entrance. I tried to keep my eyes on the surroundings, but it was impossible to sit this close and not feel his annoyance at having to do something for me for once. I gritted my teeth and glanced over at him.

"So … You had a date last night?" I asked, trying to sound casual.

He nodded briefly.

"Anyone I know?"

"No," he said.

Oh, an actual word. Wonders will never cease.

I had promised myself that I wouldn't ask, but as he turned into the street where the hospital was, the words just slipped out.

"Whatever happened with that girl you were seeing last summer?"

He glanced over at me, looking a little confused. "What girl? Do you mean Helen? She went back home to California."

"No, not Helen." I had forgotten about her. But sure, there had been more than one girl last summer, that was right. But then, where did Laura fit into all of this? "The Johnsons' daughter, next door. What was her name?" I pretended to search my memory, even though I remembered it well. "Linda? Lisa?"

"Laura," my son corrected me, and I studied his face carefully to see his reaction when he spoke her name. "I wasn't seeing Laura. She was just … around."

I could tell that he tried to seem casual, but there was a tension in his voice that hadn't been there a moment ago. Talking about Laura made him uptight, for some reason. Why was that, I wondered. Especially if she hadn't been his girlfriend.

"What do you mean … around?" I asked. We were almost at the hospital, and I found myself eager to know.

Jonas shrugged. "You know … There are always girls who are crushing on the lifeguards. It's like having groupies. Like we're rock stars or something."

I regarded him cautiously. "But she was never your girlfriend?" I asked, just to make sure. Not that it made my lusting after her any less creepy, but it sure would help to know that Jonas hadn't—Oh, don't even think about that.

"Laura. Hell, no." He pulled up to the curb right outside the emergency entrance. I didn't get out of the car.

"What do you mean, hell no?" I frowned

and studied his face. He seemed tense, still. Annoyed. Even more than usual, I mean.

He scoffed and waved dismissively with one hand. "Fat chicks, man," he said, his voice dripping with contempt. "Why would I, you know?"

I felt the taste of vomit in my mouth and swallowed hard. The urge to punch that awful brat straight in the face had never been this overwhelming, but there were people all around, and the last thing I wanted right now was to be arrested for assault.

Without saying a word, I pushed open the car door and got out. Limping toward the entrance, I could hear the car pull away, but I didn't turn to look.

It was painful to admit, but at that moment, I actually hated my own son.

5

LAURA

I HAD SPENT all morning indoors, flat out on the couch in the living room, surfing the web, and watching YouTube videos of stunning and talented people doing incredible things in beautiful surroundings.

Depressed, me? No, why would I be?

Almost everything in my grocery bag had been ruined, either by soaking up the tomato juice and disintegrating into a bloody pulp, or by being shredded by the glass shards. In the end, I just had ice cream for lunch. It must have been a sign of how miserable I felt that I didn't even enjoy it. I had checked the Messenger group every hour or so, but none of the girls had been online all day.

Well, of course not. They were busy. They had lives. They had jobs, adventures.

Eating ice cream on an empty stomach made me slightly queasy, and as I dragged myself upstairs to fetch my phone charger, I wondered how long a person could live like this.

There was a small round window on the landing that had a narrow view of the street, and just as I passed it, I saw a taxi pull up. It looked like the same taxi I had arrived in yesterday, so I did a double-take, but then I saw that it was just the same company. Just as I started up the stairs again, the back door of the taxi opened, and a man stepped out.

It was him. Mr. Lindstrom. Jonas's dad.

I stopped a couple of steps away from the window, where he hopefully wouldn't see me. He had his back toward me as he closed the door, but when he turned toward his house, I could see his face clearly. He looked miserable, and as he started walking, I noticed that he was limping. That was strange. He had been fine this morning.

In the middle of the street, he stopped and looked over at my house. My heart stopped for a second, but he didn't seem to be looking at the window where I was, just at the house in general.

Why would he do that? I had hoped that he'd just forget that he'd seen me and not say anything to Jonas or anyone else.

Even with the miserable frown, he was a handsome man, and it was obvious where Jonas had gotten his good looks. The fact that he had seemed so … kind hadn't hurt either. Those stunning blue eyes had looked at me as if he honestly cared.

I felt something swell and ache inside of me. If only that had been true. This summer could have been so much easier to get through if I'd had someone in my life who actually *cared*.

Someone to talk to. Someone to have dinner with. Someone who would lend me a shoulder to cry on so that I didn't have to be alone with all of my worries.

Picturing myself in Mr. Lindstrom's arms, sobbing onto his broad shoulder as he wrapped his strong arms around me, provoked a weird reaction. Not so much the feeling of comfort and paternal support that

I had expected, but rather … So many feelings that I couldn't even name. Weird. I felt almost tingly, and I hadn't felt that way since … well, forever.

He had crossed the street now, and I leaned forward to catch a last glimpse of him before he disappeared out of sight. He lifted one hand to open his garden gate and then looked over toward me again. He stopped and frowned, looking worried.

Was he worried about me?

In that case, he was the only one who was.

Pushing back from the window, I made my way up the stairs. The charger was by the bed where I had left it. I stood for a moment in the doorway staring at the unmade bed. It seemed to be calling me. Get back into bed, it seemed to say. It's not as if you've got something better to do today. Might as well sleep the day away.

Shaking my head, I crossed the floor, grabbing my charger. Then I pulled off all my clothes and found an over-sized T-shirt with a faded print that I put on instead. I might as well work on my tan. The sun ought to have reached the back patio by now.

Walking back downstairs, I couldn't help myself. I stopped at the small window and looked out onto the street, at the spot where Mr. Lindstrom had appeared.

It was so weird that the first guy to make me feel anything other than bad would be the father of the guy that had made me this miserable in the first place. For so long I hadn't even wanted to think about being with a guy, and now …

Now, I was thinking about it.

But not just any guy.

I was thinking about *him*.

It was a silly schoolgirl crush; I knew that. The girls would laugh at me if I told them, I knew that, and I immediately resolved to never tell them anything at all about the handsome Mr. Lindstrom. They would giggle and then move on. And this didn't feel like a giggling matter.

If fantasizing about Jonas' dad could somehow repair some of the damage that Jonas had caused last summer, then perhaps that was a good thing?

But it was a good thing that would need to remain a secret.

I had never told the girls about what had happened between Jonas and me, so I couldn't very well explain to them what I was going through. They might not have the perfect love lives, and none of them had a boyfriend at the moment, but I didn't think they would be able to understand what I was dealing with.

It was better to just keep it to myself.

And fantasies were allowed. They were harmless.

No one would ever need to know.

PULLING the lounger out to the edge of the patio brought me into the sun, and I removed the T-shirt and made myself comfortable. The warmth from the sun started seeping into my cold and stiff body. It felt healing on more than one level.

I reached my arms over my head and stretched to relieve some of the tension. There was a lot of it, in my neck, back and shoulders mainly, but just being out here in the sun made me feel a little better. I just needed to relax. All this stress wasn't going to help me sort anything out. And I had a lot of things to sort out.

My future, for one.

I had never really had a dream profession or any particular goal, apart from the standard princess and/or air stewardess career plans that almost all girls had at one time or another. Heather had known from an early age that she wanted to be an artist, but I had never had anything like that. Felicity and I had been united in our waywardness, but we had comforted each other and reassured each other that it was going to be fine. We would find our dream job one day. There was plenty of time. We were still so young.

And it hadn't felt like a pressing matter as long as we were still in school. I don't know how it was with Felicity, but I had managed to keep all thoughts of the future hidden away in a dark corner of my mind all through college. As soon as I had graduated, those stressful thoughts had burst out of there like a zombie mob on a rampage and taken over all of my faculties.

Now, it was all I could think about, and not in a productive 'let's make a plan' kind of way.

More of a debilitating 'I don't have what it takes, I'm not going to make it' kind of way.

With a heavy sigh, I rolled over onto my stomach and checked my phone again.

Still no updates from the others.

And I certainly didn't have anything new to rapport, so I wasn't going to post anything.

I rested my head on my arms and closed my eyes. There was the slightest of breeze and it felt nice against my bare butt. Thank goodness for high fences and thoughtful architects that had built these houses with completely private back gardens.

I might not have a bright future ahead of me, but I was going to have the perfect all-over tan when this summer came to an end.

PELLE

I HAD SPENT all morning at the hospital, waiting to get my ankle x-rayed, but in the end, it had turned out to be nothing more than a sprain. Perhaps I should have been grateful for that, but my ankle was still swollen and painful, and my mood had not improved since my exchange with Jonas in the car.

On some level, I knew that a lot of this had to do with the pain and the discomfort, but on another level, I was prepared to throw my own son out onto the street and cut him out of my will for what he had said about Laura.

I just didn't feel like I could live with

anyone that I felt such contempt for, even though he was my own son.

Feeling stressed about work, I hauled myself up all the stairs and into my office, but once I'd sat down behind my desk, I didn't seem to be able to focus on anything at all. All I could think about was that beautiful girl, those large sad eyes staring back at me from under that hoodie.

What was it that had made her so upset? Was it just that I had come running toward her? I knew that this was an issue with women in public spaces, that many of them felt unsafe and vulnerable because of a few bastards who gave all of us men a bad rap, but ... there had been something else, I was sure of that. She hadn't been scared, or at least not *just* scared. There had been a sadness there, something soft and vulnerable, that had made me want to wrap my arms around her and comfort her in every way I could.

Ironically, my cock seemed to be the part of me that was the most eager to do the comforting.

I snorted at my primitive reaction and

shook my head. Yeah, that's what a pretty young girl like Laura would want when she was feeling sad. A dirty old man trying to get into her panties.

But she's not even wearing panties, my cock reminded me, most unhelpfully.

Now I was definitely not going to get any work done.

I grabbed my phone and found the footage from yesterday. I should delete this, and not just from my phone but from the cloud storage backup as well. And I intended to. I just …

I watched the whole thing a couple of times, and the part where she rolled over and showed herself to me in all her glory made me almost teary-eyed.

Not to mention rock hard.

Annoyed, I put my phone down and pushed myself out of the desk chair. Limping over to the window with the view of the Johnsons' garden, I told myself that the pain I was feeling in my foot was a suitable punishment for my nasty thoughts. It had been a one-time thing, surely.

But no.

She was there. Again.

Naked. Again.

On her belly on the striped lounger, presenting her round peachy mounds toward me in all their glory. I didn't know if I should laugh or cry.

In the end, I just unzipped my jeans and reached into my underwear. Slowly, I started tugging and I felt the pressure build. My intensely unhelpful brain supplied me with a ton of B-roll, of all the things I could possibly think of doing with such a wonderfully beautiful young woman. And a few things I wouldn't even dream of doing …

I was on the brink of coming when Laura rolled over onto her back. At first, I thought that it was the perfect view to get me to the peak, but then my eyes widened as her hand slid down between her legs and started to move back and forth.

Oh. My. Fucking. Glory.

I was on the verge of exploding, but my hand just stopped mid-tug, and I stared at Laura as she masturbated slowly, gently, right before my wide-opened eyes. Oh, this was unreal. I wondered what she was thinking of when she touched herself like that but realized that I probably didn't want to know.

It didn't matter. I got to watch. And it was the most mind-blowing experience of my life. Seeing her back arch and her head toss from side to side, her toes curling as she crested the same peak I had paused on the brink of.

"Oh, Laura," I groaned silently, squeezing my cock hard, feeling it twitching against my palm.

But instead of finishing myself off, I let my erection soften in my hand, staring at the most beautiful woman I had ever seen as she climaxed all alone on a sun lounger.

I knew that I would never be the man of her dreams, but it seemed as though she didn't have anyone in her life right now that could give her what she needed. And I would be happy to be that guy for her, even if it was just for this summer. Older men and younger women weren't anything unusual. Perhaps she would be open to the idea of a little summer fling. She needed someone. I needed someone.

But I couldn't just ring her doorbell with my cock in my hand and make her a generous offer, though. I would have to find another way to approach her. Preferably some way that let me get a sense of whether or not she'd be interested in a little summer dalliance.

As she curled up on one side, satisfied but lonely, down there in the sun, I started to formulate a plan.

As soon as Jonas had left for his afternoon shift down on the beach, I made my way over to the house next door. My foot was a bit better, but I kept up the limp anyway, in case Laura could see me through a window somewhere.

I rang the doorbell and waited, leaning against the porch railing.

It took a long while before there was some movement inside. The curtain on the small window next to the door twitched, and then … nothing.

I was starting to think that she wasn't

going to open, but after what felt like an eternity, I heard the deadbolt turn. She only opened the door a few inches, peering out at me.

"Hey, Laura," I said.

"Mr. Lindstrom?" she said. The door might have opened another half an inch or so, but no more than that.

"How are you doing?" I asked, trying to sound calm, but in reality, my insides were in turmoil. She had been crying. It was obvious. And the idea of her being all alone in that big house and crying with no one to comfort her was … devastating. It wasn't right.

"I'm fine," she mumbled.

"Good," I said. "Good, good …" I glanced over my shoulder toward the beach. "Have you been out for a swim yet?"

She shook her head. "No."

Nothing more.

"I was wondering," I said, "what your plans were for the summer. Are you going to be here a while?"

She frowned a little. "I don't know. I don't really have any plans." She was staring at the porch while she spoke, at the weathered boards between our feet, but now she glanced up at me. "That's kind of why I'm here," she continued. "To figure that out."

"Oh?" I raised my eyebrows in what I hoped would signal a request for more information.

"I just graduated from college," she explained, "so I'll have to find a job."

I nodded. "I see." I tried to meet her gaze, but she quickly looked away. "What kind of job are you looking for?"

She shook her head, and I could tell that part of the sadness had to do with her unemployment. "I don't know. Anything. Whatever."

I wanted to grit my teeth at that statement. Whatever. It was my absolute least favorite word, especially when it came from the lips of someone young and bright with all the options in the world at their feet. How could they all be so … indifferent about life? Didn't they have dreams? Hopes? Anything.

Pushing my frustrations to the side, I gestured to my bandaged foot. "Well, while you're trying to find a job, perhaps you could do some work for me?"

She looked up at me now. Then a quick glance over at my house before she resumed her study of the floorboards. "I don't think that would be a good idea," she mumbled.

"Why not?" I asked, using all my self-restraint to not show my rage over my son and his asinine comment. "Is it … because of Jonas?"

She didn't look up. Just shook her head slowly. "Did you tell him that I was back?" she said, and her voice sounded so fragile that it hurt.

"No," I hurried to say. "No, you asked me not to, so of course I didn't."

That brought the ghost of a smile to her lips. "Thank you."

"Jonas doesn't have to know," I said. "You don't have to meet him if you don't want to."

She glanced up at me now, and there was something in her eyes that made me worry about what Jonas might have done to her. Perhaps there was something more than just cruel comments about her weight.

"I sprained my ankle when I was out running this morning," I said, "and I'm going to have some problems getting around over the next couple of weeks." Actually, I was already feeling much better, and the doctor had told me that I'd probably be able to go running again by the weekend, but Laura didn't need to know that. "It would be a huge help if you could run some errands for me, help out around the house and stuff like that." I could tell that she was going to say no, so I hurried to add some incentives. "Just when Jonas isn't around, of course. And I'll pay you. Whatever you think is reasonable."

I didn't think that money would sway her; after all, her dad was Fletcher Johnson, but I was surprised to see her biting her lip as if she was considering it.

"If you think it might work without me having to run into Jonas," she said. "I'm happy to help."

I could feel my face split up into a happy grin and hurried to tone it down. Play it casual, dude, or you'll scare her off.

Stupid old wolf, showing off his teeth.

"Great," I said. "Jonas has an early shift tomorrow. Come by any time after ten, and you won't run into him."

She finally met my gaze. There was something so vulnerable in her eyes, something so sad, that I just wanted to cross the porch and take her in my arms.

But that would only have scared her away.

"Thank you," she said. "I'll come by tomorrow."

I didn't want to leave. At that moment, everything inside of me just screamed at me to go to her, to comfort her, to show her that men could be trusted and could be useful to have around if you had certain urges.

Oh, I'd love to show her everything I knew about men and women.

Instead, I pushed away from the railing and made my way down the steps. "See you in the morning," I said over my shoulder, exaggerating my limp down the garden path.

And the idea of doing that absolutely brightened the rest of my day in a way that was almost disconcerting.

You'd almost think that I had a crush on the girl.

LAURA

THE NEXT MORNING, I waited by the window on the landing until I saw Jonas leave for work. He looked just as I remembered him, down to the same surf shorts and bomber jacket that were the local lifeguards' uniforms. His hair was a little different, but I didn't think that he'd changed. Not enough that I would ever want to see him again.

I saw him disappear over the dunes and then waited for at least ten minutes, in case he'd forgotten something and had to double back. Even though I knew he was gone, I still had my heart in my throat as I made my way over to Mr. Lindstrom's house. It was about the same size as my parents' house, but a completely different architectural style. I remembered my parents discussing it, my mom thinking it was an eyesore, and my dad thinking it was cool. I took my dad's side of the argument, as usual.

I was startled when the door opened before my finger had even left the doorbell. Mr. Lindstrom must have been waiting for me. The idea made the tingle inside of me even more pronounced, and I pushed the thoughts from my head.

This wasn't about a stupid crush. Mr. Lindstrom was hurt, and he needed my help.

And I needed Mr. Lindstrom's cash.

I wasn't sure exactly what he did for a living, but I knew he was loaded. Even if I hadn't heard my mom's jealous comments, I'd have been able to tell from the inside of his house. It was gorgeous and grand and filled with expensive furniture and gadgets.

"How's the foot?" I asked to try and distract myself from the weird feelings that had started spreading throughout my body as soon as I saw him.

He grimaced. "Hurts like h— a lot," he corrected himself with an apologetic smile.

If I'd had any stupid fantasies of a summer fling with the older man next door, those fantasies would have been extinguished by that comment. It was obvious that he thought of me as a little girl, not as a grown woman. Part of me was saddened by that realization. Several parts of me, in fact.

Just being in his presence made it clear to me what a man he was. His stature, his voice, his scent, they all conspired to intoxicate me and fill my head with all kinds of … ideas.

"What do you need me to help you with?" I said. Looking around, I could tell that he must have a cleaning service or a housekeeper, because there wasn't a speck of dust or a single dirty coffee cup that needed washing up.

"What can you do?" he replied and limped over to a bar stool by the kitchen island, resting one butt cheek on it. "What did you study in college?"

I shrugged. "This and that."

I hadn't really gotten around to choosing a major. Instead, I'd just taken whatever class had seemed the most interesting at the time. Altogether, I'd learned a bunch of stuff, just not anything that seemed to be of any use in the workplace. All the negative thoughts that had followed me around since graduation suddenly seemed to grow more intense.

"This was a bad idea," I said, gesturing at the squeaky-clean kitchen island. "I thought you needed help with tidying up or something, but you obviously have someone to do that. If you need someone to do *actual* work of some kind ..." I didn't even know what business he was in, so I couldn't hazard a guess as to what he might consider work, "... then I'm sorry, but I'm not your girl." I tried to keep a straight face, but to my great shame, I could feel my bottom lip start to tremble. "Don't get up," I said, "I'll show myself out."

I was halfway to the door when I heard his booming voice behind me. "Laura, get back here!" I don't know why, but my feet just stopped, despite the fact that I desperately wanted to leave. I slowly turned around and forced myself to look at him.

There it was again. The caring that laced those blue eyes and made them absolutely lethal. Oh, Laura, stupid girl. You have a crush on Jonas's dad.

"Please don't leave," he said, and my feet stayed put. "Just … stay a while. I'm sure we can figure something out." He nodded toward a state-of-the-art coffee maker. "Would you like some coffee?"

I sighed. Perhaps I was overreacting. If I wanted him to treat me like an adult, I had to stop acting like a little girl. "Sure. Some coffee would be nice." He started to get up, but I stopped him. "No, let me."

I walked over to the machine and studied it. It was a completely different set up than what I was used to from The Grind, but I could see how it worked. It was an advanced model that delivered everything you could want in a hot beverage, both through manual settings and through pods. I sighed. Why would you get a machine like this if you wanted your coffee to taste like bathwater?

"There are some pods in the cupboard just above the machine," Mr. Lindstrom said behind my back. "I'll have a cappuccino, but there are plenty of other flavors if you prefer something else."

I glanced at him over my shoulder, one eyebrow raised. "You drink pod-coffee when you have a machine like this?"

He shrugged. "It's ridiculous. I have never been able to figure it out. Just grab a couple of pods. It's fine."

I snorted. "Please. Just …" I waved dismissively at him and opened the cupboard. As I had expected, there were not just pods there, but also a bag of whole coffee beans and a grinder. I opened the bag and sniffed. The intense aroma made me smile. I glanced over my shoulder at Mr. Lindstrom again. "I'm going to make you the best damn cup of coffee you've ever had," I said, and then I busied myself with the settings.

It took a few minutes, but when I had made us both a cup and placed his on the kitchen island in front of him, I was feeling a bit better. Not as frantic, not as frightened. Doing something that I was good at had restored at least a fraction of my confidence. Now, we could have a cup of coffee, talk about the weather, and then I could leave, calmly and without causing a scene. It was obvious that he didn't have any work for me, but I would still like to enjoy this brief moment together with another human being.

I hadn't realized how intensely lonely I'd been until I was in the same room as another person. Someone who looked at me appreciatively and sniffed at his coffee cup.

He took a small sip and tasted the coffee with an intense concentration. Then the small frown disappeared, and his whole face lit up. "This is amazing." He stared at me and then at the machine before looking at me again. "How on earth did you do that? I've never been able to make anything that even remotely resembled coffee on that blasted machine."

I smiled and took a sip of my own cappuccino. "I worked at a coffee place for a couple of summers." The smile widened when I remembered The Grind and my shifts there with the girls. I put the cup down and looked up. He was looking straight at me, and my knees almost buckled.

What was that even, in his eyes? Admiration? It couldn't be. No one had ever looked *admiringly* at me. Not ever. This was so weird.

"You're amazing," he said. "This is the best coffee I've ever had."

I snorted. "Great," I said, a little despondent. "At least I have a career as a barista to fall back on if I can't figure out what I want to do with my life."

He held his cup between both hands. "And what would be wrong with that?" he asked.

I frowned and turned my cup in a semicircle. "It's not a real job," I said.

He looked surprised. "You perform a service and get paid, isn't that the definition of a job?" he asked.

I laughed a little. "Well, in that case, I could just be a hooker. It pays a lot more per hour," I joked but instantly regretted it.

Something shifted in his eyes, and I couldn't really tell what he was thinking, but I couldn't imagine it was anything good. He must be embarrassed for me, that I didn't know what to say or not say in polite company.

He leaned forward and looked me straight into the eyes. "Whatever you decide to do with your life, Laura, I have no doubt that you are going to blow them all away with your awesomeness."

I stared back at him, a million emotions crowding around inside of my chest, each of them clamoring for my attention. None of them made any sense. I didn't know what to say. Instead, I just burst out crying.

Burying my face in my hands, I made a herculean effort to pull myself together enough to say goodbye and leave, but before I could manage to get a grip, I felt someone right next to me.

Mr. Lindstrom had gotten up off his stool and walked around the kitchen island, just to comfort me. On his sprained ankle! I wanted to be strong enough to tell him that I was fine and that he should go and sit down, but … I wasn't.

At that moment, I was all kinds of weak.

He put his arm around my shoulder, and I let him pull me into his broad chest. His embrace was everything I had imagined it to be, and more. His arms were just as strong as I had expected, but his scent had a completely different quality when I buried my face against his shirt and slipped my arms around his waist. I could still smell his cologne, but also something else, something more appealing, more natural, something that must be his own scent.

He's just being kind, I kept telling myself, but there was nothing in the world that could make me push him away; not in a million years was I leaving his embrace as long as he was willing to offer me his comfort. It felt a thousand times better than I had imagined it, and the comfort was real, sincere. It was seeping inside of me through his soft shirt, and my body and soul soaked it up like a dry sponge.

One of his hands was rubbing my back in a small circular motion, and the other was holding me tight, pressing me against his solid body. I felt my body meld into his, my soft curves fitting into his hard angles as if we'd been made for one another. With a deep sigh, I let go of all the sadness and all the worries. Right now, right here, I didn't have a thing to worry about.

I knew that everything was going to be all right as long as I could stay in his arms.

The hand that had been rubbing my back

slid up along my spine and neck and came to rest on my cheek. I tilted my head backward and looked up at him.

"Oh, Laura," he said, and it sounded almost as if he was in pain.

What was I going to say back? Oh, Mr. Lindstrom? That would just sound weird!

But in the end, I didn't need to say a thing because he leaned forward and placed his lips on mine, effectively silencing me for several minutes.

His kiss was intense and exploratory, tinged with hunger and something that I thought was passion. During a split second, my head was filled with the nightmarish memories from last summer, and I gripped his shirt, prepared to pull him off me, but then I felt all the ways in which this situation was different, and the fear and panic slithered away into the dark corners of my subconscious.

This was nothing like last summer. One, I was sober. Two, this felt good, great even. My whole body was responding to his eager caresses and the intense kiss in a way I had never thought I would experience again.

Slowly, tentatively, my body started to feel like mine, and the intense sadness that I had hauled around for the last year suddenly lifted.

I had forgotten that it could feel this way, letting someone this close. That other people might want to give you pleasure, and not just use you for their own.

But … Mr. Lindstrom?

A hug, that I could understand. But this was something completely different.

Shifting in his arms, moving even closer, I felt his arousal pressing against my stomach. No, this was not just my imagination running wild. That was an actual erection. A real, live, rock hard cock straining the fabric of his trousers. It should have been intimidating, but who was I kidding? My body responded violently, but not with fear, oh no. With enthusiasm. With eagerness. With a warm wetness that throbbed with longing.

Never mind that it was 10.30 in the morning, and I was standing in my neighbor's kitchen, having a cup of coffee. Not exactly the perfect scene for a seduction.

But it was exactly what I needed right now.

Something that would make me feel better, about myself, about my body, about my life.

The last time a man had pressed his erection against me, I had screamed and struggled to get away.

This time, I fumbled with the buttons in his fly to release that monster of a cock, in the hope that he would use it as a magic wand and make all the bad things that happened last summer disappear.

Oh, Mr. Lindstrom.

Please make it all better again.

PELLE

I HADN'T PLANNED THIS.

Or, rather, I hadn't planned for it to happen in exactly this way.

I had *hoped* it would happen, eventually. And I had hoped that it would be as great as I had imagined it, every time I thought about her, which was pretty much all the time.

I had been resolved to take my time, talk to her, get to know her. Figure out what had made her so sad and what I could do to make it better.

But when she suddenly started crying, I had to go to her. I had to comfort her.

Just a hug. That was all. I never intended it to lead to anything more than that.

Stupid of me, I know. Because as soon as I had her in my arms, I knew that I never wanted to let her go. She felt so right there, so soft and warm and luscious and absolutely perfect.

There were a few too many layers of fabric in the way, but we could do something about that. I had been prepared to wait a while, but before long, I felt her hands searching for the buttons on my jeans, and their eager fumbling was almost more than I could bear. Her lips tasted of coffee and mint and some kind of lip gloss, and every time I broke free to catch my breath, I felt myself pulled back in for more. It was all just exactly what I needed right now. I would never have thought that I could be what *she* needed, but judging from her eager moans, this seemed to be the case.

Oh, this was going to be good.

I contemplated carrying her upstairs to my bedroom but didn't think my ankle could take it. Instead, I wrapped my arms around her and moved us both across the floor over to the large sectional in the living area next to the kitchen. She followed my lead and made no objections when I lay her down on the soft fabric, pushing a couple of throw pillows to the floor. On the contrary, she was tugging at my shirt and pulled it off over my head before letting her hands explore my bare chest on their way down to my open button-fly. One of her hands disappeared inside of my jeans, and I had to grip the backrest of the sofa hard and think of soccer to keep from exploding right then and there.

This wasn't going to be over in a minute if I had anything to say about it. I intended to take my time with her.

Her dress was a soft, silky fabric with broad shoulder straps and a wide skirt that had slid up around her hips as she lay back and pulled her bare feet up on the edge of the couch. Her naked thighs were smooth and tanned and even more perfect than I had ever imagined. I ran one hand down on the inside of one of them, and she lifted her hips toward me, steering my hand to where she needed it to be.

I smiled and leaned over her, claiming her lips once more as my fingers found the damp fabric of her panties and rubbed it gently.

She made a little noise and lifted her hips again.

"Oh, Laura," I whispered. "I'm going to make you feel so good, don't you worry about a thing. It's all going to work out, you'll see."

She stared up at me, and I thought that I could spot a glimpse of doubt in her large, beautiful eyes, but then she closed them and leaned her head back, baring her long, slender neck.

I placed a row of kisses along that neck, down over her clavicle toward those magnificent breasts that had haunted me since I first saw them. Tugging the fabric of her dress to the side revealed a naked breast, a large round peak with a dark brown aureole and a stiff nipple pointing straight at the ceiling. I just had to taste it and wrapped my lips around it at the same time as I slipped a couple of fingers inside of her panties. She gasped and grabbed my hair at the back of my neck, clasping it tightly. It hurt in the best possible way. Running my tongue around her nipple as I circled her clit with my index finger provoked another gasp, and again, she lifted her hips toward me.

I reluctantly let go of the delicious nipple and looked up at her as I continued my slow massage.

"You are magnificent," I said, my voice hoarse. "Just … perfection."

She opened her mouth to say something, but as my finger slipped inside her wet folds at that exact moment, no coherent words came out. Her eyes rolled back inside of her head and her lips moved as if she was uttering a spell.

If she was, it was working on me, that was for sure. I had never been this hard for this long, and I still didn't feel the need to plunge inside of her to find my release. We had all day.

I shifted down the couch and placed myself strategically between her legs that were spread as wide as they could go. Pulling her panties to one side, I found her hard clit with my tongue and worked it hard. She tilted her pelvis toward my face, and I tasted her salty juices dripping from my fingers that were buried inside of her warm cave, massaging the front wall of her glorious pussy.

The thin strip of hair that I had seen from my office was golden and gleamed in the light that came pouring in through the large windows toward my garden. Where that strip ended, her light pink folds opened up for me like the petals of a beautiful rose. She was glorious, and I had never seen anything like it.

Sucking in her clit hard and letting the tip of my tongue brush over it brought her to the edge fast. She was mumbling something incoherent and her head was tossing from side to side. She was going to come any second now.

I had to feel it from the inside.

I quickly pulled my jeans down enough to free my throbbing shaft and moved up the couch until I was positioned at her entrance. Her eyes had been closed, but she opened them now, at first just a glimpse, but then they widened at the sight of me. She opened her mouth to speak, but I couldn't wait to hear what she had to say. There would be plenty of time for us to talk later, but right now, I just had to bring this girl to climax before we both spontaneously combusted.

Pushing deep inside her wet pussy, made us both groan out loud. I plunged all the way in, and she welcomed me by wrapping her legs around my hips. She tried to hold me in, but I pulled out as far as I could go, just for the pleasure of thrusting deep inside of her once again. Her eyes were still wide, but they were blurry and unfocused from the intense feelings we had unleashed in one another.

I couldn't hold back any longer. Bracing myself with one leg on the floor, the sprained ankle, smart Pelle, I grabbed the backrest of the sofa and just gave her all I had to give. Quick hard thrusts as deep as I could go, grinding my pelvic bone against her clit every time I reached the hilt. She felt magnificent around my cock, and when she pressed her fingernails into my buttocks, I just couldn't take it. It was too much. She was too much.

Looking her straight into the eyes, I finally managed to find a connection, and that was what brought us both to the crest and beyond. I pushed and pushed until I felt her muscles clench around my rigid shaft, and then I collapsed on top of her, my cock convulsing inside of her warm wetness.

I just barely had the energy left to kiss her one last time before I rolled off her and pulled her close. She felt limp like a ragdoll in my arms, warm and soft and magnificent, and I wished I had the energy to tell her.

I intended to, as soon as I had gathered my strengths.

9

LAURA

I WAS LYING in his arms, completely mellow and high on bliss and endorphins when I heard the front door open.

It took forever, or at least a couple of seconds, before my brain managed to put two and two together and come up with the answer: Disaster!

Only two people lived in this house. I had just had the best sex of my life with one of them. And the other one was the one person in the world that I never wanted to see again.

Oh, let it be the cleaning service, I pleaded wordlessly as I pushed Jonas's dad away from me and flew up off the couch. But no.

"Dad?" someone shouted from the hall-way. "Are you home?"

Pelle sat up and looked toward the door-way. I snagged his T-shirt from the floor where I had thrown it and passed it to him. It only took him a second to pull it on and an-other to get up and button his jeans. Running one hand through his hair made him look as if nothing had just happened here.

I glanced around after a mirror or some other reflective surface. The floor to ceiling windows worked just fine, now that it sud-denly had become dark outside. I glanced up toward the sky as I tried to un-tousle my hair. It was pointless. My whole appearance just screamed JBF.

Just Been Fucked.

My tousled hair, the wrinkled dress, my red, swollen lips, and confused, dazed look were all dead giveaways.

Jonas was going to know what had hap-pened here as soon as he saw me.

Pelle moved toward the kitchen island where we had left our coffee cups. I hurried after him on weak legs. Please, don't come in here. Please, just go to your room first, to drop something off, so that I could slip out the front door and not be seen. Please, please, please.

But just as I slipped in behind the kitchen island, Jonas appeared in the doorway. Broad-shouldered and imposing, he frowned when he saw me standing there. I quickly picked up the coffee cup and took a long sip. It was cold. Not lukewarm. Cold. How long had we been …? Never mind.

"You're home early," Pelle said, and I was amazed at how casual he managed to sound. I didn't think I'd be able to form a coherent sentence.

"They've closed the beach," Jonas said to his father, but his eyes were still directed at me. "There's a storm on the way in."

"Really?" Pelle said. "Well, we were just having coffee. You remember Laura, right? From next door?"

Jonas nodded slowly, and his gaze finally left me and moved over to his father. I put the coffee cup down and tried to look as if nothing out of the ordinary had just happened. In reality, my insides were in turmoil, and I wanted nothing more than to just run out the door.

If only Jonas hadn't been standing right there, blocking my only escape route.

He came into the kitchen, toward us, and with every step he took, my heart rate increased. I did not want him to come anywhere near me. Just being in the same room was unbearable; increased proximity was going to be torture. Every nerve ending in my body was standing at attention and not in a good way. Just a few moments ago, all I had been able to feel was pleasure and arousal.

Now, it was fear. Disgust. Shame. Panic. And did I mention fear?

"This was nice, Mr. Lindstrom," I heard myself say, and my voice sounded shrill and fake. "But I've got to run. Thanks for the coffee."

Keeping my distance to Jonas, I moved in a semicircle toward the door, not looking back, just raising one hand in a wave when Pelle said my name. I couldn't do this. I couldn't be here. It was all just too much. There wasn't enough room inside of one person's head or heart for this many conflicting emotions.

As soon as I was out of sight of the two men, my legs buckled under me, and I had to grab hold of a doorpost out in the hallway to stop myself from collapsing in a puddle on the stone slab floor. A thunder knell cut through the silence, and at the same moment, angry rain started to pelt the windows. It looked almost completely dark outside, even though it was the middle of the day. I pulled myself away from the doorpost and forced myself to keep walking toward the front door. It felt like it was miles away, but even all the way over by the front door, I could still hear the voices from the kitchen.

"What the *actual* fuck?" Jonas said, and his voice was dripping with contempt. "Have you gone completely pedo or what? She's even younger than me!"

"You watch your mouth!" Pelle replied, and his voice was trembling with rage. "This is none of your bloody business."

Jonas laughed, a short burst of cruel laughter. Completely heartless. I recognized it. It was the same way he had laughed that night. At me, that time as well. That laughter had haunted my nightmares for the last year, and I didn't think I would ever forget it. That particular nightmare hadn't ended when I woke up the next morning.

I dragged myself toward the door, desperate to get out of there before the emotions brought me to my knees.

"Not my business? That slut is everyone's fucking business, and I mean it literally. She'll spread her legs for anyone. Or any*thing*."

I could barely breathe as I grasped the door handle and tugged at it. The door seemed to be locked, and I couldn't figure out how to unlock it. There had to be a button somewhere. Something.

"What are you talking about?" Pelle was growling now. The gentleness in him was gone. Perhaps for good. If Jonas told him, Pelle would never look at me with that caring gaze again.

He would never want to see me again, never want to kiss me or …

No.

Never.

Jonas laughed again. "I'll show you," he said, and his voice was dripping with cruelty. "The whole town has seen it ages ago, so I don't see why you shouldn't. You need to know what you've dipped your cock in, so that you understand why it starts to burn when you pee."

A speaker somewhere behind me sparked to life, and I turned and stared at it. It was mounted high on the wall, in the corner. I hadn't noticed it. Now it was emanating disgusting sounds. Cruel laughter. My voice. My slurring, disjointed voice. I could hear the same sounds coming from upstairs and from inside the kitchen. There had to be speakers all over the house.

"Give it to her," some guy shouted. "Let her have it."

A chorus of male voices cheered.

"She's gagging for it," someone else shouted. "Oh, watch out, I think she's going to …"

Disgusted groans sounded as if they came from all directions. Then they all laughed again. I don't know how many they were. I had no actual memories of the events in the movie, and everyone there had been careful to stay out of frame of the single phone camera that had recorded it all. Someone had sent me a copy of the video clip the next day. One of the guys. Probably Jonas, although he hadn't sent it from his own number.

I never knew who the other guys were. None of them showed their faces on camera. It was dark, but the flash on the phone had lit up the object of the recording.

Me.

It wasn't a very long clip. Two minutes and forty-three seconds. But in it, you can clearly see me, lying on my back on a picnic table down by the beach. I'm drunk. Plastered. Paralytic. Someone has pulled up my dress and shoved the neck of his beer bottle up between my legs. Another generous fellow tried to make me suck his cock, but I'd gagged and thrown up on him. I hoped I had ruined his shoes, at least.

I could hear a groan from the kitchen, and it wasn't from the movie. It was Pelle. Disgusted by the sight of me and all those guys. I was sure that he instantly regretted what he had done. And we hadn't even used a condom. He would probably be off to the clinic first thing tomorrow to be tested.

The sound of his disgust finally helped me to break out of my paralyzed state, and I finally managed to unlock the front door. It almost blew out of my hand, but I managed to get it closed again and hurried down the front steps. The wind along the street was so strong that I could barely walk upright, and trash kept slapping against my bare legs as it blew along the sidewalk. I got the gate open but then couldn't close it. The wind was too strong. In the end, I just had to leave it, flapping on the hinges. It was going to break, I knew that, but I had to get inside.

Once I had finally closed and locked the front door behind me, I staggered into the living room. One of the sun loungers had blown off the patio, and I had to go outside to fetch it. God knows where it might end up if I just left it out there.

When everything was secured, I was soaking wet and completely exhausted, both emotionally and physically. I slammed the patio door shut and locked it before staggering over to the couch and collapsing there. I didn't even have the energy to get out of the wet clothes, just pulled a blanket over me and curled up into a little ball.

Even though the storm was roaring straight above me, all I could hear was my own pathetic moans from the video and Pelle's disgusted reaction.

It had been so great, but great things never lasted.

I had learned that lesson the hard way.

10

PELLE

THE VIDEO CLIP wasn't very long, just a couple of minutes, and the person who had shot it hadn't possessed any particular skills as a cameraman, but there was no doubt as to what I was watching.

My Laura being victimized by a number of young men, egging each other on to commit one humiliating act after another on that poor defenseless girl.

Shock gave way to anger, an explosive rage that homed in on its target like a heat-seeking missile. My son. The rapist.

"You absolute bastard," I roared. "Get your disgusting ass out of my house." I raised my clenched fists to demonstrate my willingness to help him find his way to the front door. "I do not want to see your face ever again, and you can be sure that I will be contacting the police about the crime I just witnessed on that screen."

Jonas looked baffled, not scared, and then he burst out laughing. "Yeah, what crime is that? Having some fun with a fat slag. Sexual misconduct with an ugly broad? Last I heard, that was not illegal in this country."

I was on him in a flash, the thin fabric of his life-guard jacket crumpling in my raging fists. "Sexual assault is, though. And I will make sure that every one of those coward friends of yours goes down for this too. You disgusting pieces of shit!"

He looked a little worried but pulled himself up and looked me in the eye. "I don't know what you're talking about. No one assaulted anyone. She wanted it; she said so. She asked me to meet her that night. She drank the beer I gave her." He pushed me away, brushing the wrinkles from the front of his jacket. "And she never pressed charges or even mentioned the police or assault or any of that bullshit. She loved it. She's a horny little bitch and will do anything for a fuck." He stared at me, his mouth twisted into a contemptuous sneer. "As you well know." He looked me up and down and shook his head. "So pathetic. Fucking a schoolgirl. What, are you having some sort of midlife crisis or something?"

I saw red and realized that I needed to be careful. I might hurt the little shit if I gave in to his taunting. "I mean it," I said between gritted teeth. "You need to leave here, now. And never come back."

He snorted. "Yeah. Like … where am I supposed to go in this weather?" He made a gesture toward the floor to ceiling windows that were streaming with rain. A flash and then another knell of thunder.

I just stared at him, feeling all the anger and disgust boiling inside of me. "I. Don't. Care." I said, pausing in between every word for emphasis. "But you are *not* staying in this house." I crossed my arms and spread my legs in a decisive stance. "If you are not packed and out of that door in fifteen minutes, I am calling the police."

He snorted again but with less bravado

this time. "You're psycho, man," he protested. "I'm not—"

"You are *not* welcome here," I interrupted him. "I don't ever want to see or hear from you ever again. Leave, and don't come back."

He stared at me, perhaps for the first time realizing that I meant it. Then he turned and walked out the door, turning right into the corridor that led to his suite of rooms. I let my arms drop and felt them tingle as I released the tensed muscles. I could have killed him. Perhaps I should have.

What kind of monster was he that he could do something like that to a girl?

I could taste blood and iron and walked across to the windows staring out into the storm. The viciousness of the rain gusts was nothing compared to the violent emotions that blew through my mind and my heart.

What had I done?

That poor girl had been through hell, and I had pushed myself onto her, perhaps making it all worse. She must be traumatized by the events in that video clip—I knew that I was traumatized just by watching it—but I hadn't cared about any of that.

All I had cared about had been to satisfy my own primitive needs.

I felt sick and heartbroken as I glanced over at the couch. It had only lasted for a short while, but every moment of our intimate encounter was ingrained in my mind forever. It had been beautiful. Intense. Magical.

Surreal.

But perhaps only in my mind.

What had been going through Laura's head as I pushed myself inside of her, without even having the decency to use protection? There was no way of knowing for sure, but I could make an educated guess. My forceful thrusts must have re-awakened all kinds of trauma in that poor girl's head. Perhaps even scarred her for life.

I rubbed my face with both hands. This was awful. Contemptible.

How was I going to live with myself?

Jonas appeared in the doorway behind me. I could see his silhouette in the reflection in the glass in front of me.

"I'm going," he said grumpily.

I didn't reply. What was there to say? I

didn't care where he went, only that he didn't stay here. I didn't care what happened to him. Not after what he had done.

He might be my son, my flesh and blood, but he was dead to me.

I made a mental note to call my lawyer and have him removed from my will and my life insurance. I had put up with too much for too long. And as long as his arrogance and smugness had only been directed toward me, I'd accepted it. It wasn't strange that he'd grown up to be a bit of a prick. His mother had poisoned his mind from day one, and I hadn't been around.

I had thought that I owed him for not being there, but as of this moment, I considered my debt repaid in full, with interest.

I didn't owe him anything anymore.

"What about … my allowance?" he asked, and I could tell that he tried to sound casual, but his voice was thin and a bit shrill. He was uncomfortable.

Good.

"I'm not giving you another cent," I said, still facing the window. I couldn't stand to look at him. He disgusted me.

"But ..." He paused, and I could see his reflection in the glass next to me sort of deflate. He looked smaller, suddenly. "And the car?"

"I'm canceling the lease," I said. "Return it to the dealership by the end of business on Monday."

"But what am I supposed to do?" he said, taking a step inside the room and reaching out his arms in a pleading gesture.

I slowly turned and looked at him. "I. Don't. Care," I repeated. "Go to hell, as far as I'm concerned. I hope you struggle. It's the least you deserve after what you did."

He looked confused. "I didn't do anything," he said and sounded almost offended. "I didn't touch her. I wouldn't."

The taste of vomit rose at the back of my mouth. "Get the hell out of my house," I said slowly. "And never come back."

He looked angry. "She's not worth it, you know. She's just a stupid girl. There are tons of them, hanging around. You have no idea what it's like, being a lifeguard."

I stared at him, seeing him and all his flaws and defects clearly for the first time.

"She is not stupid," I said slowly. "And there is no one like her in the world." I took a step toward him. "What you did was appalling and disgusting, and I will speak to my lawyer about possible criminal charges. Now, get the fuck out of my house. I'm not telling you one more time. You either leave, or I throw you out."

"But …" He gestured toward the large windows. "There's a storm …"

I shook my head. "I don't care. I don't ever want to see your face around here, ever again. And you make sure to tell your buddies that I will see to it that they all pay for what they did."

He looked worried now, for the first time. "But you didn't mean what you said, right?" he asked, and his voice was thin now. "About not giving me any more money? I am your son, after all."

I gritted my teeth. "Not anymore, you're not." I raised one hand and pointed toward the door. "Now, leave."

He stared at me for a moment. But then he left. I heard the roar of the tropical storm outside as he opened the front door, and then silence as he slammed it shut.

I was alone.

He was gone.

But this wasn't over. Not by a long shot.

11

LAURA

THE STORM RAGED all through the day and well into the night. I didn't notice it, though. Where I lay on the sofa, trembling and distraught, it was the inner turmoil that occupied my mind.

The shame and humiliation over what had happened last summer. And the shame and humiliation over what had happened this morning.

For a brief time, in his arms there on the couch, I had allowed myself to think that somehow, everything was going to be fine. Everything was going to work out, through some miracle.

It was stupid of me, I know.

How do you even begin to repair something as shattered as my life? There was no way.

But during our intense encounter there on his large sofa, I had felt something inside of me start to mend. I had begun to reclaim parts of my body that I had been rejecting for so long.

Perhaps, if it could have lasted a bit longer, I could have managed to put a few more pieces back together.

Now, I would never know what might have been.

I lay there, curled up into a fetal position, face against the wall, and tried to remember all the details of the brief time we had spent together—really together. But every time I tried to recall the way he'd touched me, the memory was overshadowed by memories from last summer. Vague, nightmarish images that hadn't made any sense until someone had sent me the footage of what had happened that night on the beach. And the feeling of Pelle pushing inside of me, joining us into one, was tinted with a miserable sheen because I couldn't stop thinking of that beer bottle and how sore I'd been when I woke up the next morning. I'd been bleeding, even though it wasn't that time of the month, and there had been bruises on the inside of my thighs. My mouth had tasted of beer and something else, something chemical. I'd known as soon as I woke up that something terrible had happened, and I'd kept bursting into tears all day, pulling away from my parents and not picking up the phone when Felicity called in the afternoon.

I'd spent almost all day in my room but was sitting at the dinner table with my mom and dad when my phone buzzed on the table next to me.

"Laura!" my mother had said reproachfully. "We're in the middle of dinner. Put that thing away."

I'd only had time to glance at the screen and see that I'd received one new message from Unknown Caller before I'd slipped the phone into my pocket. Not until I had retreated to my room again after dessert had I opened the message.

The video clip had started playing automatically, but the screen had been so dark that I hadn't been able to tell what it was at first. It had taken almost a full minute before my brain made sense of what I was seeing.

Me. Completely plastered, on my back with my legs spread wide on top of the picnic table down by the beach where the lifeguard guys liked to hang out and drink beer after dark. I knew I'd been there last night, still had the text from Jonas where he invited me to join him there, but couldn't remember a thing after getting there and accepting a plastic cup of beer from one of his mates.

I wasn't much of a drinker, apparently. I had been embarrassed about the fact that I hadn't been able to hold my liquor, but this …

This was so much worse.

I watched the clip three times, just standing in the middle of the room, my feet nailed to the floor. The third time I saw a faceless guy walk around to the top end of the table, unzip his jeans and push his groin into my face, my stomach did a backflip, and I had to grab the wastepaper basket by my desk to avoid vomiting all over the off white carpet. I didn't remember any of it but seeing his hips jut forward and his jeans hang low on his scrawny hips, I thought I could feel his cock push against the back of my throat.

I still felt like gagging whenever I thought about it. Could still taste the vomit.

I had made up some excuse and gone back to Seattle the next day. I hadn't told my friends that I was back early. Instead, I had spent the rest of the summer break alone in my parents' house.

The last weekend of the break, I had pulled myself together and gone to meet the girls for a back-to-school reunion. I had done a great job of pretending that everything was fine, and no one had been able to tell. Heather had wondered in passing why I wasn't more tanned—not that strange, considering I'd spent the last three weeks in my room—but I had changed the subject, and no one had mentioned it again.

A whole year had gone by, and I had thought that I had been able to put what happened behind me. Returning to this place had brought it all back with a vengeance.

Perhaps it's true what they say. That you can't run away from your past.

I couldn't run at all, right now. The darkness that had followed me around over the last year had enveloped me completely and was pulling me down, dragging me under. The brief glimpse of something good, something amazing, made it all so much worse in contrast. I don't know that my crush on Pelle would have been able to save me, but the brief time we'd spent together had been a well-needed respite from all things gloomy and depressing.

But it had all been an illusion, and this was my reality.

My dark thoughts were interrupted by a banging noise. Something was thumping against the glass doors to the patio.

At first, I thought I would just ignore it. I couldn't manage to get up off this couch, not now.

Then I realized that the storm was even louder than before, and if there was something out there that had come untethered, it might break the glass. And then, what would I do?

Gathering the very last dregs of my strength, I pulled myself off the couch and staggered toward the door. I only made it a couple of steps before I stopped cold.

Because on the other side of the glass stood Pelle, legs wide to brace himself against the horrific gusts, arms raised against the glass. He was soaking wet, and the rain was dripping from his fringe, down over his face.

"Laura!" he bellowed, but I could barely hear him over the storm.

I couldn't move. Just stood there, staring at him. What was he doing here? What on earth had possessed him to go outside in this weather? He could get himself killed—

The idea of him getting harmed in some way finally broke my paralysis, and I hurried over to unlock the doors. He slipped inside, and we both had to push with all our combined strengths to get the door closed again. As soon as the lock had clicked shut, I felt the adrenaline-fueled energy drain from my body and my knees buckled. Pelle caught me and helped me back to the couch, where he wrapped the blanket around me, rubbing my arms to help with circulation.

I stared up at him. He was dripping wet, and cold drops fell from his hair onto my face. "Here," I said, trying to untangle myself from the blanket and give it to him. "You need this more than I do."

He shook his head and sat down on the coffee table in front of me. His jeans were so wet, they almost looked black, completely soaked through. He must be freezing. "I'm fine," he said. "I just had to come and see how you were."

I stared at him. "I'll be fine," I said automatically, just as I had done so many times over the last year, both out loud and in my own head, without believing it for a second.

He looked me straight in the eye, and I was stunned to see that the caring concern was still there, perhaps even more intense now than before. How was that even possible? I had heard his reaction to the video. I knew how he must feel about me, and if he was half as disgusted by me as I was, then he would never even want to be in the same room as me. I knew that I wouldn't want to be, if I'd had a choice. What was he even doing here?

"I'm so terribly sorry for what happened to you, Laura," he said, "and if my son had any part in what happened, I will make sure that he suffers all possible repercussions."

"But …?" I didn't understand. What was he talking about?

He shook his head and continued. "I will talk to my lawyer on Monday, but for now, I've told Jonas that he is no longer welcome in my house and that I never want to see him again."

I frowned. "He's your son." Blood was thicker than water and all that.

He grimaced. "On some level, sure. But what he did to you was inexcusable. I can never forgive him for treating you like that." He found my hands inside the blanket and held them in both of his, rubbing them for warmth. "If there is anything I can do to make up for what he did …"

I pulled away, wrapping the blanket tighter around me. This was making me uncomfortable. I didn't want to talk about what happened, and I didn't want Pelle to know.

"There's nothing you can do," I mumbled. "What happened, happened. It's in the past." He had seen that I was fine, so why didn't he leave? Why was he still here?

He looked pained. "I understand," he said slowly, and I wanted to hit him. Of course, he didn't understand. How could he? Looking into his eyes, I saw my own pain reflected back at me, and I felt sick. He would never be able to look at me without seeing that video. And knowing that he had seen it, I'd never be able to look at him without thinking about what happened.

It was all ruined. What could have been a fun summer fling had turned sour, bilious even. "No, you don't," I said. "Now, please, just leave."

But he didn't move. "I'm not leaving you alone like this," he said, and the determination in his voice brought tears to my eyes. "You can't be here all alone. Is there someone you want me to call? Your parents?" The look on my face told him no, in no uncertain terms. "Not your parents. Okay. A friend then?" I shook my head. There was no one who could help me right now. No one that I wanted to tell. The fewer people who knew about it, the better. "Well then," he said. "Then I'm staying."

I stared at him. "This isn't …" I started to say. But then I stopped. What was I trying to say? That this wasn't his problem? Surely, he knew that. I looked at him. A single drop rolled down his flushed cheek. He was trembling a little from the cold.

"You're freezing," I said.

He shook his head. "It's nothing."

"You'll catch your death."

Another shake of the head. "I'll be fine."

I sighed and looked down at myself. My dress was wrinkled after being wet and then drying as I lay huddled up on the couch. "Sure you will," I said. "But we both need a change of clothes." Another crack of lightning lit up the back garden. "The storm doesn't seem to want to let up anytime soon." I couldn't send him back outside in that weather. He would have to stay here.

I stood up, still with the blanket wrapped around me. "Come with me."

I led Pelle down the stairs into the basement where my parents had a spa. There was a sauna, a jacuzzi, and two state-of-the-art showers with all the trimmings imaginable. I pulled a folded-up guest bathrobe from the linen cupboard by the door and opened the door to one of the showers. "Here," I said, hanging the bathrobe on the hook inside the door. "Get out of those wet clothes and take a warm shower."

He didn't move. I sighed. "And I will do the same in there," I said, pointing at the other shower across the room. "Once we're warm and dry, then we can talk."

He was silent for a while, but then he nodded and stepped into the shower room.

12

———

PELLE

I DIDN'T NOTICE how cold I was until the door to the shower room had closed, and I shivered violently as I peeled off my soaked clothes. Thankfully, the water was hot, and the water pressure almost as good as in my own shower. Being pelted in all directions by steaming hot water worked wonders, and I felt myself starting to relax. What a fucked-up day this had turned out to be! I didn't exactly grieve over my decision to kick Jonas out, but I felt horrible about what had happened to Laura, and the idea that my son might be behind the whole thing made me sick.

I didn't know how I could make it up to

her, but I knew I had to try. Not because it was any of my business or responsibility, but because the poor girl didn't seem to have anyone else. How was it possible that she hadn't told anyone in all this time?

How could such a magnificent young woman be so lonely?

Wrapping the fluffy bathrobe around me, I stepped outside into the spa. The tiles on the walls were tacky and dated the room, but I thought that it wasn't a bad thing to have and considered adding a few of the features to my own cellar, next to my home gym. A sauna would be especially nice.

The door to the other shower room opened, and Laura stepped out. Her cheeks were flushed from the hot shower, and the bathrobe she was wearing must be a men's size, because it brushed the tiled floor as she walked. She gave me a wan smile, and I felt something warm spread through my chest.

"Feeling better?" I asked.

She shrugged. "And you?"

I shrugged back.

She had been coming toward me, but now she stopped a couple of feet away. Too far, my whole body screamed. I'm guessing her body screamed something more to the tune of too damn close. It hit me like a dagger to the heart, that this girl had been violated in such a way that it might influence all her intimate relationships for the rest of her life. If Jonas had been here, I would have killed him.

"Have you eaten?" I asked.

She looked confused but then shook her head.

"Come on," I said, gesturing her toward the stairs. "I'll fix you something."

"There's no food in the house," she said apologetically but walked ahead of me up to the main hallway and into the kitchen.

The kitchen was large and equipped with all the latest technology, but it didn't look as if anyone had ever cooked anything in it. I started opening cupboards and pulling out drawers. Everything you needed to make a serious meal was there but looked unused. "Your parents?" I asked. "Not that big on cooking?"

She shook her head and sat down on a barstool by the kitchen island, a huge slab on concrete with metal trim. "No. My mom doesn't see the point in cooking. She's a whiz at bossing caterers around, though."

I gave her a crooked smile and continued my exploration. In the fridge, I found a carton of eggs. The large freezer held a selection of expensive varieties of vodka, several bags of ice, and a couple of large Tupperware containers with left-over canapes.

"The eggs are past their expiration date," Laura said. "I already checked."

I pulled the carton out anyway and put it on the kitchen counter. "They're probably fine anyway," I said. "Eggs usually last way past the date on the carton." I found a glass and cracked one of the eggs in it. It looked fine, the white was clear and the yolk was round and yellow, and it smelled fresh. "See, they're perfectly edible. I'll make you an omelet."

She smiled a little, even though she still looked sad. "Okay."

Some of the canapes were salmon, and some had spring onion and cream cheese. MacGyver would have been proud of the way I incorporated them into the omelet, and Laura looked surprised when I presented her with the result of my experiment.

"This looks great," she said. "Thank you."

I had made enough for both of us and sat down across the corner of the island, so as not to crowd her. We ate in silence while the storm roared overhead. She finished almost all of it before pushing the plate away.

"Thank you," she said again. "You can leave now."

I didn't move. "I'm not going anywhere," I said. "You shouldn't be alone right now."

She flinched but hid it well. "It's ancient history," she said, not looking at me. "For you, it just happened, but for me it happened a year ago."

I regarded her closely. "From what I can tell," I said slowly, "it's still happening to you."

I could see that it pained her. That I had hit a nerve. She pulled herself together, a herculean effort. "Still, it's happening to *me*," she said in the end. "It's not your responsibility. You don't have to stay."

"But if I want to," I said. "Can I?"

She looked at me now, and her beautiful

eyes were tinged with confusion. "Why would you want to?" she asked, almost angrily. "It's not anything to do with you. You're not responsible for what Jonas did."

I didn't know what to say. How to explain to her that I felt protective of her. That I felt drawn to her, physically but also on a whole other level. I didn't just want to continue the explorations from this morning, until I had learned everything about her body and what gave her pleasure. I wanted to know everything about her. What her dreams were for the future. What her favorite color was. What kind of music she liked.

How could I explain that I hadn't been able to focus on anything else since I'd seen her there on the sun lounger? Oh, I must never tell her about that! This poor girl had been violated enough.

"No," I said, after thinking for a while. "I'm not responsible for what Jonas did. I don't want to stay because of him. I want to stay because of you."

She looked confused, still. "What happened between us this morning ..." she said, and I could tell that she was struggling to look unperturbed, "I understand if it was just a … one-time thing."

I looked at her, seeing her there in the kitchen in the over-sized robe, but also remembering her on my couch, cresting the climactic peak and clenching around my cock. "Do you want it to have been just a one-time thing?" I asked, hoping, praying, begging wordlessly to please don't say yes.

She didn't reply at all. "I know that you saw the video," she said after a while, and her shoulders slumped.

I nodded. "I figured. I heard the door slam behind you." I shook my head. "I'm sorry I didn't follow you right away. I … It took me a while to find my footing. Get Jonas out of the house and all that. I wasn't thinking straight. I should have come here first." I reached over the concrete surface and placed my hand on her arm, gently, not holding on. "I'm sorry that it took me so long to understand what was more important." She didn't pull away, and I took that as a good sign.

She stared down at my hand on her arm. "How can you still want to touch me?" she croaked, her voice completely fractured, "after seeing what happened?"

I let my arm slide down the long sleeve and then slip inside it, stroking her naked arm underneath as far up as my hand could fit. "What happened between you and me this morning," I said, "felt so right. I don't think I've ever experienced such intimacy with a woman I just met. It affected me deeply, profoundly." I leaned forward, careful to give her room to move away if she felt the need. She didn't. "I am disgusted by what those guys did to you, and I'm going to do everything in my power to make sure they are punished for it. But listen to me now, Laura. *I am not disgusted by you.*" I squeezed her arm gently. "I am fascinated by you. Enthralled by your beauty. Inspired by your strength. And fiercely attracted to you on every level, body and soul." She was staring at me now, and I looked her deep into the eyes. "The only reason I'm not trying to seduce you right now is that I don't want to push you into something that you're not ready for. I don't want to tear up any old wounds."

Her eyes welled up with tears, and I felt her pain like a stab in my own heart.

"I've been telling myself that I'm fine," she whispered.

"But you're not," I replied gently.

"But I'm not," she echoed faintly.

"Have you talked to anyone about what happened? Told anyone?"

She shook her head.

"So, no one knows?"

Her face was distorted by pain. "Everyone knows," she said silently. "That video had thousands of views."

It took all of my self-restraint to keep my anger in check. Those boys were going to pay for what they had done to my Laura.

And that's what she was, I realized. *My* Laura.

Never mind that we didn't know each other. That's we'd only just met and succumbed to a moment's impulse and fierce attraction. Perhaps it wasn't for life—I was too old for her, she was too young for me, et cetera—but it was definitely not for just one hurried tumble on a couch.

I wasn't done with her. And I hoped that

she wasn't done with me either.

"I'm going to make them pay," I said. "You're not alone in this anymore. I intend to stand by you in this."

She looked away. Perhaps I had gone too far. Fine. I would back off.

There was just one thing I needed to know.

"This morning," I said, "I hope I didn't hurt you. I certainly didn't mean to."

She glanced at me, a faint smile just at the corner of her lips. "Don't worry," she said softly. "You didn't hurt me at all." Another smile. "Quite the opposite, actually."

I felt an immense relief coursing through my body. "Good." I squeezed her arm. "I'd never want to hurt you, Laura. I hope that you know that. If I'm coming on too strong, just tell me, and I'll … I'll back off."

She glanced over toward the windows. The storm seemed to have started to abate. "It's still raining," she said. "But it seems to have calmed down a bit. In another hour or so, you should be able to go home."

I studied her face. "Do you want me to leave, Laura?"

She looked confused, sad, and confused. "Do you want to stay, Pelle?"

I nodded. "I want to stay here with you," I said and hoped that she could hear the truth in that statement. "I want to make sure that you're all right before I go."

The confusion gave way to something else, and she placed her other hand on top of mine. "Do you want to make it all better?" she whispered.

I nodded, completely speechless as she tugged at the belt on her robe and let it fall open, revealing her gorgeous naked body underneath. Its soft, velvety skin pulled at me like a strong magnet, but I held back, afraid that I would hurt her, somehow.

"I want to make it all better," I confirmed. "I want to make it all right. But I'm worried that you're not—"

I didn't have time to finish the sentence before Laura slipped off her barstool and came toward me, all naked and warm and welcoming.

It was not the reason I had come here, but I wasn't about to say no.

I would never be able to say no to Laura.

LAURA

I COULDN'T BELIEVE what I was hearing. Was it possible that he wasn't appalled by me after seeing that disgusting movie? His hand was on my arm, all light and soft. Caring and comforting, not demanding or pushy or any-thing at all aggressive.

I was broken inside; I knew that. But our brief time together this morning hadn't felt like it was tearing open any of the old wounds. On the contrary, it had felt healing.

Like he could make it all better.

It was strange but appealing, the idea that he might be able to make me forget all the bad things, all those horrible feelings that those boys had made me associate with my body. Perhaps he could make me reclaim my sexuality, somehow.

It was certainly worth a try.

I expected him to recoil when I undid my bathrobe and moved toward him. Talk is cheap and all that. But he didn't. Not at all.

His warm hands reached out for me, slipped inside the bathrobe, and pulled me into his strong embrace. I expected to feel a bit panicked when he held me tight, but I didn't. I felt safe.

I couldn't remember the last time I'd felt that way, but it brought tears to my eyes. I leaned my head against his shoulder and wept silently as he slowly rubbed my back with one hand. He kissed me lightly on my temple and whispered in my ear.

"My beautiful Laura. My magnificent, gorgeous girl. You don't have to carry this secret alone any longer. I'm right here with you."

I turned my face toward him. "Stay with me," I whispered.

He looked me straight in the eyes. "I'm not leaving you," he said. "Not until you tell me to."

I took his hand and led him up the stairs to my bedroom. As I crossed the threshold, I spotted the wastebasket by my desk and thought that I could smell the vomit, even though it was a year ago and I'd cleaned it out with bleach at the time. For a moment, I faltered, but then I kept going, over to my queen-sized bed. It was unmade, but Pelle didn't seem to mind. He slipped his hands underneath my bathrobe and pushed it off the shoulders. It fell to the floor, and his followed. We stood there next to the bed, just looking each other in the eyes, completely naked. The storm kept pelting the windows, but it seemed to be a little lighter outside. The worst had passed.

He leaned forward and kissed me gently on my lips. It was a tentative kiss, but not reticent. He wasn't doing it because he felt he should. He wanted to. I slipped my arms around his waist and pulled him closer, shivering a little even though the room was warm. His desire was obvious, and I felt a warm tingle as he pressed his erection against my stomach, almost apologetically. I could understand that he'd want to hold back, that he'd be concerned about hurting me, but all I could think about was how good it had felt when he had pushed inside of me. It didn't have to be bad. Men didn't have to be cruel. They could be gentle. Caring and considerate. Loving, even.

Of course, I knew that he didn't love me. We didn't even know each other. This was purely physical. But I was fine with that. This felt like exactly what I needed—something purely physical but positive that would help eradicate all those dark memories. I wanted to forget all about those boys. Wanted to feel good again. And Pelle could help me with that.

Pressing my stomach against his erection, I opened my mouth a little to let his tongue in. His groan of pleasure resonated inside my chest. Eagerly, I got up on the bed and pulled him with me. Standing on my knees on the crumpled sheets, I kissed him intently, passionately, and felt my hard nipples rubbing against his firm chest. One of his hands was on my bottom, kneading my flesh, and the other was moving slowly up my waist toward my breast. When he finally reached it, his lips stopped moving for a moment, as if he couldn't manage both at once. I broke free from the kiss and leaned back to give him a better look. His eyes shone with desire and something more. Almost a kind of worship.

"Oh, Laura …" he said, and there was something almost pleading in his voice. "I want to make it all better for you, but I don't know if I can."

I smiled at him and placed one hand on his cheek. "You can." Then I let the hand slide down his neck, over his chest and stomach and down to his groin. His erection should have seemed intimidating, perhaps even frightening, but it didn't. I felt completely safe in the knowledge that he wouldn't use it to hurt me. Wrapping my fingers around the solid shaft, I watched his eyes widen. "You can make it all better," I said, my voice hoarse with desire. It was boiling inside of me with an intensity that surprised me. I hadn't thought that I'd be able to enjoy sex ever again, but this morning had taken me by surprise. Would it be as good this time, perhaps even better? We had time. A proper bed. And all my dirty secrets were out in the open.

The fact that he knew the worst thing about me and still wanted me was incredibly arousing. I had felt so dirty for so long, but now I felt cleansed. Purified. And it was all thanks to him.

Moving my hand up and down his thick erection, I felt strong for the first time in such a long time. Like I was in charge of what was happening to me. I felt invincible and was determined not to let what had happened stand in the way of my future any longer.

But as I sank down onto the mattress, getting ready to wrap my lips around his cock, I felt the old panic starting to rise inside of me, chasing away the desire. I couldn't do it.

Not yet.

Instead, I lay down on my back, looking up at Pelle, who was still on his knees. He didn't seem to be in a rush. He took his time, watching me where I lay, all naked and exposed to his admiring eyes. I managed to push the panic out of my mind and reached for him. He crawled on top of me, standing on all four, looking me straight into the eyes.

"If you don't feel like you want to do this, just say so," he said earnestly.

"I want to do this," I said, and my voice may have sounded weak and helpless, but that was just because the emotions were so overwhelming when he was this close.

He bent down and kissed me again, thoroughly. I placed my hand on the back of his neck to pull him down on top of me, but he stayed on all fours and soon broke off the kiss. He moved further down, placing a row of kisses all the way down my neck, across my clavicle and onto my chest. He paused and looked up at me as if seeking confirmation before he wrapped his lips around my stiff nipple. My hand slid up into his hair, feeling its soft, silky texture, gripping him hard, holding him in place.

He was bearing his own weight on one arm, while the other moved down my stomach and slipped down between my legs. My pussy felt hot and throbbing and the relief when he found my clit and started to rub it was immediate. Yes! I could do this! I could feel myself slowly starting to return to who I had been before. No, it would never be as if those horrible things had never happened. But it could be good again.

With Pelle, it could be great.

I lifted my pelvis against his hand, eager for more, faster, and he smiled at me as he let my nipple slip out of his mouth and tickled it with his tongue. "Do you want me to go on?" he asked, his voice hoarse with desire. "You have to tell me what you want me to do, Laura," he said. "I won't do anything that you don't want me to."

I felt like screaming at him, but instead wrapped my legs around his and tried to pull him down on top of me. "I need to feel you inside of me," I said pleadingly. "I need you, Pelle."

He nodded calmly. "You will, baby. You will. I just need to make sure that you're ready for me." A couple of his fingers slipped inside of me and I whimpered. It felt so good, and I knew that he could feel that I was more than ready for him.

To my intense frustration, Pelle moved down my body, placing kisses in a zigzag line down my stomach and on the inside of my thighs. No! I wanted his cock inside of me! I groaned and arched my back. But before I could protest, his lips and tongue had found my clit, and I lost the ability to express my desires in coherent speech. Instead, I just let go and allowed the sensations to spread throughout my body like ripples on a still pond. With his fingers inside of me, I was rapidly accelerating toward that glorious peak that he had already brought me to once today, but I didn't want to come like this. I wanted to come with him inside of me. The way the tip of his tongue tickled my clit with featherlight movements back and forth had completely deprived me of any articulation, so the only thing I could do was to throw my head back and scream out my feelings as they rose to an impossibly high peak.

It felt as if I was floating a couple of feet above the mattress as pink stars started to appear at the edge of my field of vision. Everything went black, and I could hear myself screaming as if from a place far away.

When I came to, Pelle was again standing over me on all four. He was looking down on me with such affection; it made my heart soar. "Laura, baby," he said. "Are you all right?"

I think I managed to nod. My body felt completely relaxed and mellow and everything was pure bliss.

He smiled at me. "Do you still want to feel me inside of you?"

I didn't think I could take anymore, but my inner muscles contracted at the thought of him, so I smiled and spread my legs wide, reaching for him. For a moment, just as he was positioning himself right at the entrance, I flashed back to that video, to that beer bottle, but looking up into Pelle's eyes, that image just popped like a balloon and vanished from my consciousness. This wasn't anything like that. This was Pelle and me. Here and now. It had nothing to do with anyone or anything else.

He slid inside of me, slowly, gently, and I grabbed his hips and pulled him deeper. He fit so perfectly that I sighed with happiness and wrapped my legs around his hips, holding him in place. He didn't seem to be in any hurry.

"My Laura," he was muttering right next

to my ear. "My glorious, beautiful Laura. You have no idea what you do to me."

I wrapped my arms around him and held him tight. No, perhaps not. But neither could he imagine what he did to me.

I didn't think I could express it in words, but what I did know was that it was all kinds of good. This was perhaps just a summer fling, but it was a healing experience, and I intended to enjoy it for as long as it lasted.

He started to move, found a good pace, and I pushed up to meet his every thrust. After two such intense orgasms on top of the day I'd had, I didn't think I had any more to give, but as he increased the pace, I could feel myself racing him to the peak. His face looked strained but determined as he pushed himself deep, over and over.

"Oh, yes," I whispered. "Just like that. Right there. Right …"

And then everything was exactly that.

14

PELLE

Two weeks later:

I was sitting in my office one morning, staring at the screen of my MacBook Pro. There were numbers on there, good numbers, even, but I didn't see them. My eyes kept being drawn over toward the window where the sun came streaming in.

This summer hadn't turned out at all as I'd expected.

The house was quiet now that I had it all to myself. And I hadn't been working nearly as many hours as I usually did. I didn't seem to be able to focus on work. There was something else that was occupying my mind, day and night.

I closed the laptop and walked over to the window. Looking down into the garden next door, I saw her immediately. She was lying on the sun lounger, right on the edge of the patio. I still hadn't told her that I could see her from here.

Perhaps I ought to.

Glancing back at my desk, I decided that it was a much too nice day to be stuck in the office.

Perhaps I should get some sun. After all, what was the point of living in Florida if I was going to spend all my time in the office?

I almost ran down the stairs and out my patio doors. The gate in the tall fence was usually kept locked, but I had unlocked it two weeks ago when I'd gone to check on Laura to make sure that she was OK.

She hadn't been. But I had made her feel better.

Opening the gate, I knocked on the wood of the fence to notify her of my presence.

She lifted her head from her arms and glanced over her shoulder. "Hi," she said, giving me one of her knock-out smiles.

"Hey, you," I said, walking over to her sun lounger.

She was lying on her stomach, her head on her arms. The lines from her bikini bottoms were barely visible after two weeks of naked sunbathing. Her skin was a lovely golden tan, and I imagined that it would feel sweet and salty if I licked it. Instead, I sat down on the edge of the lounger. She shifted a little to make room for me, but her round hip still pressed against me. As always, being close to her drove me wild.

"I thought you had to work today," she mumbled, her eyes closed again.

"I did," I said. "I just thought I'd see how you were doing."

"Hard at work on my tan," she said, and a small dimple appeared next to her full, red lips as she smiled. I smiled back, even though she couldn't see me.

"I can see that," I replied. "It's sweaty work."

"M-hm," she said.

A bottle of sunscreen stood on the patio. I picked it up. "Have you applied sunscreen?" I asked. "The UV is high today."

"I did," she replied, "When I came outside. It's probably time for some more." She opened her eyes and lifted herself up onto her elbows, regarding me over her shoulder.

"Allow me," I said, holding up the bottle.

She lay back down, and I opened the bottle and poured out a generous amount of the sticky white liquid into the palm of my hand. Rubbing it between my hands to warm it up, I then leaned forward and smeared the sunscreen over her shoulders. Her skin was warm to the touch and completely smooth. I applied a generous layer working my way down her back. She groaned appreciatively.

I took another palm-full of cream and applied it to the back of her legs, working from her feet up. Long before I reached her round naked buttocks, I was rock hard. Filling my palm for the third time, I applied the sunscreen to her smooth, round butt cheeks, massaging them thoroughly. Letting my hand slide over her bottom and down to the top of her thigh, I found her soft folds. She was wet and warm and lifted her hips toward me.

"If you want me to rub lotion on your front, you'll have to roll over," I said.

She opened her eyes and turned to her side, her glorious hip curving to a peak right beside me. Her full breasts were tanned and perky, the nipples hard and erect. I started to lean forward to taste them, but she stopped me. Her eyes were on my crotch, where my cock was pressing hard against the fabric of my shorts.

"Well now, Mr. Lindstrom," she said seductively. "If I didn't know any better, I'd think that you were happy to see me."

"I am always happy to see you," I said truthfully. I had seen a lot of her over the past two weeks, and our summer fling was in no way starting to fizzle out. On the contrary, the more time I spent with the lovely Laura, the more I wanted to be with her. "Actually, that was what I wanted to talk to you about."

"M-hm?" she said, moving toward me, still with her eyes fixed on my crotch. Her hand found a gap between my T-shirt and my shorts and slipped down inside of them.

Feeling her fingers on my aching erection made me groan out loud. "What about it?"

Before I could reply, she had released my cock from its fabric prison and pulled it out into the sun. I just barely had time to see its swollen tip glisten in the sunlight before she leaned forward, and it disappeared into her mouth. I almost came then and there but managed to hold it back by wrapping my fingers so hard around the frame of the sun lounger that it hurt. Laura took me deep and sucked me hard and completely without reservation. It was at this moment that I knew that she had put the events of last summer behind her at last. The assault had been present every time we had come together over the past two weeks, but right now, I knew that it was just her and me, for the first time. And it was magnificent.

Just before I was going to spurt straight down her throat, I pushed her away. She lay back down on the lounger, still on her stomach, and as I climbed on top, I remembered fantasizing about exactly this that first day when I had seen her from my office. Pushing inside her and pressing up against her smooth, warm buttocks felt a million times better than I'd ever been able to imagine, and as I brought us both to another one of our many magnificent simultaneous orgasms, I thanked whatever powers had brought this wonderful woman into my life.

As I collapsed on top of her, shuddering from the strength of the climax, I whispered in her ear. "I wanted to ask you if you'd move in with me."

She didn't reply, but I saw the corner of her mouth curve upward in a contented smile. Her inner muscles contracted around my cock. I took that to mean 'yes'. I might not be getting as much work done as I had planned this summer, but something told me that it would be the best summer of my life.

THE END

Curious about what Laura's friends are up to this summer? Find out in their own novellas:

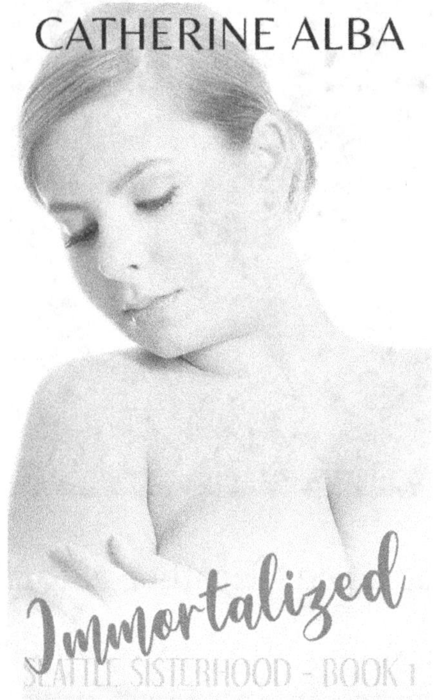

Immortalized - Felicity's story:

Staying behind in Seattle while my friends set off on great adventures was not the way I had planned to spend the summer after graduation, but here I was. Alone in a crappy apartment, working at the same old job that I'd had every summer since high school. This was going to be the worst summer ever!

Ravished - Heather's Story:

Traveling to Italy to study art and paint had always been a dream, but I had never expected to go there alone. Venturing out from the bustling city of Florence into the Italian countryside to find more authentic motifs for my paintings, my journey took an unexpected turn, literally. Surprisingly, my Italian adventure turned out to be a lot more monastic than anyone—least of all my friends back home—would have expected. I mean, Italian men do have a certain reputation, after all.

HEATHER

LESS THAN HALF AN HOUR AFTER leaving Florence, I was convinced that I wasn't going to survive this car journey. I just didn't know what was going to kill me first. The suffocating heat that was making my entire body sticky and itchy? Or the frantic Italian drivers that didn't seem to care a delicious fig about lanes, speed limits, indicators or blind spots?

The Autostrada had four lanes in both directions, and all eight lanes were packed with huge thundering lorries that were hurling along way over the speed limit. A million little Fiats and Seats were buzzing all around my equally minute rental car like a swarm of flies. Since I hadn't been able to figure out the air conditioning unit, I had rolled down the window, and the stench of exhaust fumes and the noise from the surrounding traffic was overwhelming all my senses. The sweat was trickling from underneath my breasts down over my belly and the only good thing about this day was that there was no one else in the car to see me in this state.

Why, oh, why had I decided that an excursion into the Tuscan countryside would be a good idea on a scorching hot day like this? And why had I insisted on going alone? Everyone I had spoken to I Florence had told me to stay in the city, or to take the train if I wanted to explore more of Italy. They had warned me about Italian drivers and their fatalistic approach to road safety. Had I listened? Of course not.

Yep. I was going to die here. And it would be my own fault.

My grip on the steering wheel hardened

when I suddenly saw five of the small Italian cars line up, side by side, in front of me. Sure, there were only four lanes, but hey, their cars were small enough to fit half-a-dozen across the Autostrada, so why not?

Because that is not how you do things! a part of my brain wanted to scream. Checking all the mirrors, I squeezed into the lorry lane on the far right. It was cramped and the tall lorry in front of me meant that I couldn't see anything at all up ahead, but my exit had to be coming up soon and I didn't want to wait until the last minute.

I debated getting off the Autostrada early, just to get away from this madness, but I didn't want to waste all of this lovely sunlight driving. Smaller roads would probably be less frantic than this, but it would take me that much longer to reach my destination, so I was determined to tough it out. I could do this! Surely it couldn't be much further.

At that exact moment, my phone chirped into life on the passenger seat. The car probably had a built in GPS, but it only spoke Italian, and it had been as uncooperative as the A/C. "At the next exit, take right" my phone said. I breathed a sigh of relief and flicked on my indicator signal. Finally!

Leaving the Autostrada wasn't as big of a relief as I had expected. The traffic turned out to be almost as intense on the smaller country roads, and there were a lot more distractions to take into consideration. I bit my lip and leaned forward, peering at the signs at a crossroads. My phone had told me to take a right turn, but the signs seemed to indicate that I should continue straight ahead.

I decided to obey my phone and hoped it wouldn't lead me too far astray.

It wasn't until I had taken a couple more turns onto incrementally smaller and smaller roads that I found myself alone on the road and could finally begin to calm down. The inside of the car was still sweltering, but the open window let me experience all the enticing scents of the Tuscan countryside. It was intoxicating and I stopped regretting going on this adventure. This was going to be a great day. I would get to see so much that I would never have experienced in Florence.

It was a pity that the road was so winding

and unpredictable because that meant that I couldn't see much of the scenic surroundings. The small glimpses I got here and there made my fingers itch to pull out my paints. Everywhere I looked, there was something that I desperately wanted to capture on canvas. Tall pointy cypress trees standing in attention down a ruler-straight side road. A picturesque farmyard with lush flower boxes decorating the dilapidated house, and chickens wandering casually around the front yard. A single pair of trousers on a clothesline. The round, rolling hills stretching into eternity in varying shades of greens and blues under the crisp morning sky. An ancient village on a hilltop almost gleaming with a dull orange terracotta sheen in the sun, looking exactly as it must have done 500 years ago, as if I had driven through a portal when I exited the Autostrada and traveled back to the renaissance.

"At the next turning, take right," my phone said, bringing me back to the 21st century, and I sat up and started scanning the road ahead for an exit. I couldn't see any side road, but there was a sharp curve up ahead that blocked my view. The exit must be right around the corner.

I had slowed down significantly by the time I came round the bend, and that was fortunate, because right in the middle of the road, just in front of the exit, was an animal. A large and rather dirty goat, chewing slowly and regarding the approaching car with complete indifference. I slammed my foot on the brake and one hand on the horn, before swerving over in the opposite lane without even having time to check the mirrors. Fortunately, I was alone on the road and I avoided being crushed into a pulp by an Italian lorry.

*Un*fortunately, the goat was startled by the sound of the horn and bounced away across the gravelly tarmac, straight into the path of the skidding little Fiat. I turned the wheel again, trying desperately to avoid hitting the panicked goat, and with my heart in my throat I felt the tires lose their grip on the gravel-covered tarmac. The back end of the small rental started to slide toward the edge of the road, and I panicked. Twisting the wheel back and forth and stepping hard on the brake did not make the small car stop. Instead, it started to spin around, while still sliding toward the opposite side of the road.

"At first opportunity, make a U-turn, and then turn right," my phone said, but I didn't know which way was right anymore. Everything was spinning, my head, the car, the surrounding trees.

And then one of the back tires slipped off the edge of the tarmac, and the small car tipped off the road and down a steep slope. I screamed, but if there was anyone around who heard me—apart from the traffic-obstructing goat—I didn't see them. All I could see through the windscreen was the clear blue Tuscan sky. The engine whirred and branches snapped and cracked when the car rolled backward through some bushes and then finally slowed down as the ground leveled out, coming to a stop with a low thud.

I stared at my hands gripping the steering wheel as I listened to the ticking noise from the car's engine and the whooshing sound that was the blood pulsing in my eardrums. My heart was racing, but as it slowly dawned on me that I was unharmed, and that the car had stopped its wild careening down the slope, it started to slow down. I took a deep breath and loosened my grip on the wheel. My fingers felt stiff and cold, despite the heat. After the intense noise that had surrounded me just a moment ago, the silence down here was deafening.

I switched off the engine and looked around. The car had plowed backwards down a steep slope covered in brambles and bushes. I could see the path it had taken. Somewhere up there was the road. I turned in my seat and looked behind the car. There was a field. Some cows were standing under a tree in the middle of the field, looking at me with obvious disinterest in their eyes. The car had been stopped by the fence surrounding their field, a rusty barbed-wire affair that looked like it had been there for a hundred years or more. The brambles and bushes must have slowed the car down. That fence would never have withstood an out-of-control car. Not even this tiny Fiat.

Rubbing my face with trembling hands, I took stock. I was fine. The car was fine. The goat hadn't been hurt. The cows were fine. Everyone and everything was fine.

Apart from the fact that the car wasn't on the road, where it was supposed to be. It was nowhere near the road, and I was not going to be able to drive up that steep slope, not in this car.

Pushing my seat back, I undid the seatbelt and reached for the water bottle in the tote that was standing in the foot well on the passenger side. The water was tepid but tasted like nectar after the long thirsty drive. I made another attempt at switching on the A/C, but the small screen just kept spouting Italian error messages in red boxes, and I didn't dare click on any of the alternatives, in case it caused the car to self-destruct.

I took another sip of the lukewarm water and looked around.

Now, what was I going to do?

The obvious answer was to call for help, but call who? I didn't know where I was, and I didn't know who could help me out of this situation. Did they have AA in Italy? And if so, would my travel insurance cover the expense of getting the car towed?

The only phone number I had added to my phone book before setting off was that of the emergency services, but … this didn't really qualify as an emergency, in my eyes. I wasn't hurt. The car might have been damaged somehow, by going through those bushes, but this wasn't exactly a car *crash*, now was it? I didn't need an ambulance, or angry Italian policemen breathalyzing me and throwing me in Italian jail for endangering the local livestock.

No, what I needed was a tow truck. Or perhaps just a farmer with a tractor or something that could pull me back up onto the road.

I glanced in the rear-view mirror at the cows that were still lounging in the shade underneath the tree. Where there were cows, there must be a farmer. All I had to do was find the farm.

I gathered my things from the console and stuffed my phone and water bottle in the tote. Then I pushed open the door and turned in my seat, but then I froze and just stared at the ground outside.

The car was surrounded by lush greenery

on all sides. I had been aware of that. What I *hadn't* noticed until just now was that the greenery in question consisted of nettles.

Tall, lush stinging nettles that grew in a wide field all along the outside of the fence.

I was suddenly very much aware of the fact that my legs were bare underneath my long, flowy skirt, and that my sandals were strappy and offered no protection whatsoever to the burning sensation of nettles.

I craned my neck and looked out the window on the passenger side, but the field of nettles continued over on that side as well, for as far as I could see.

I was trapped.

Now what?

Turning in my seat I looked up and down the field. There was no house in sight, no road, no sign of life, apart from the cows.

"How about a little help, guys?" I said, but they didn't respond. Just stared at me while their lower jaws ground away at whatever they were masticating. Grass, presumably.

I sank back against the seat with a sigh. A low engine sound passed by somewhere up there, where the road must be. A passing car.

I pressed on the horn, as hard as I could, for as long as I could stand it. When I let go, the engine sound had quietened.

Careful to avoid the nettles, I leaned out of the open door. "Hello!" I shouted. "I'm down here!" Then I listened. Nothing. "Can anyone hear me?" I yelled. Still nothing.

Leaning back against the backrest, I took stock. I was fine, but I couldn't stay here. What if no one came along, ever? Judging by the sound of passing cars, there weren't any signs of what had happened up there on the road. What was I going to do? Stay here until winter, when the nettles presumably withered down?

Rummaging through the tote, I found a single power bar and half a packet of chewing gum. That wasn't going to last me until winter. I had to find a way out of here. Maybe I could climb through the back of the car and try and get out through the trunk? Glancing over my shoulder, I hesitated. It was a tiny car, with an even tinier trunk. And I was a big girl. A big and not particularly flexible woman in my prime. No, climbing out through the trunk was not an option. I might not even be able to open the trunk with the fence in the way. No, that would have to be a last resort.

At least the car was in the shade, and I had some water. I would be fine.

Someone would come along.

Everything was going to be just fine.

MARCO

I WAS LOST in my thoughts and moving on autopilot when I spotted the car. I stopped and stared at it. A car, right in the middle of my best nettle plot. How on earth …?

Looking up the slope, I could see the path of destruction.

Damn.

People were always driving too fast around here, even on these narrow roads. They only had themselves to blame. Not that I cared.

As long as they didn't destroy my nettles.

I hung the large bucket I had brought

with me on one of the fence posts and pulled on my gardening gloves. Then I started harvesting. The nettles were at their peak right now. In a week or so they would start to go rough and the taste would change. This would be the last week that I would make my famous nettle soup this year. I would have to think of something else for next week.

The car was right in the middle of the patch, and I wasn't planning on harvesting enough that I'd have to go near it, but I decided to check that the fence hadn't been damaged. I didn't want the cows to get out.

Pushing my way through the thick vegetation, I leaned over to see the back of the car. It was pressing up against the fence but didn't seem to have broken anything. There weren't even any damage on the car, despite the rough path it had cut through the vegetation. When I stood up, I noticed that the door on the driver's side was open. That was strange. I peered inside and was startled to see that there was someone in there. Moving up along the passenger side of the car, I saw a lifeless woman in the driver's seat. My annoyance was immediately replaced by an ice-cold fear. Was she dead?

The chill in my chest made my entire body freeze and I just stood there, staring at her, for what felt like an eternity. I had to do something, but I couldn't make myself step any closer. Couldn't make myself touch her. My fingers already knew what her dead skin would feel like. Cold. Unnatural. I knew but didn't want to know. Didn't ever want to experience that horror again.

Because of the tall trees casting their shade in this direction, it was dark inside the car, but I could see her clearly. She was beautiful. Serene. At peace.

There was nothing horrifying about the sight of her. No blood anywhere. No sign of trauma. She was leaned against the backrest, her head slumped to one side so that her face turned slightly toward me. Her long, chestnut hair framed a young and beautiful face, and the deep red color of her lips was a powerful contrast to her soft, pale cheeks. I had seen death, and *that* was not what it looked like.

Moving closer to the car, I raised one hand and tapped gently on the window.

The woman startled and her eyes flew open, staring straight at me. Despite the dark hair, her eyes were a bright and unexpected blue and the intensely red lips parted in a surprised gasp.

"Are you all right?" I asked.

She just stared at me.

"Signorina? Do you need help? Shall I call an ambulance?"

As soon as I had said the words, I realized that I didn't have my phone on me. It was probably lying on my desk somewhere, buried in papers. *Those aren't papers, they are overdue bills,* the nasty voice at the back of my head chimed in, but I ignored it.

She still didn't reply, just stared at me. Then something seemed to trigger her into action, and she leaned over and opened the passenger door.

"Hi!" she said, and my eyebrows rose toward my hairline. An American? "I must have dozed off. It sure is hot today!" She fanned herself with one hand and glanced over her shoulder at the cows in the field. "Are those your cows?" She pointed toward the back of her car. "Is that your fence? Did I break it? I'm so sorry. I didn't mean to. It's just—"

"Are you hurt?" I asked.

She shook her head. "No, just a bit freaked out." Glancing down at my gloved hands, she continued, "Could you help me get out of here, do you think?"

I didn't understand. If she wasn't hurt, what was she doing, just sitting here? "Do you need an ambulance," I repeated, in English this time.

She smiled, and the smile made her already beautiful face light up from inside in a way that disturbed me. Made me angry. Made me regret having come here. Why couldn't I have decided on another antipasti for this evening? It was too late in the season for nettles anyway. What had I been thinking?

"I just need a tow truck," she said. Then she bit her lip. "Unless you've got a tractor."

I stared at her, uncomprehending. "Why would I have a tractor?"

She looked back at me, looking as confused as I felt. "Aren't you the farmer?"

I shook my head. "No, I'm not." I put one hand on the passenger door and leaned forward, peering into the small car. "If you can walk, then what are you—"

My voice broke off mid-sentence when my eyes fell on her bare legs under the steering wheel. The heat in the car had made her hitch up her long skirt all the way to the top of her thighs and the smooth-as-velvet skin reminded me of peaches in cream. I forced my eyes away from the glorious sight and looked around the car. My delicious nettles, everywhere.

"Yeah," she said. "Those darn weeds are all over, and I'm in sandals." She looked at my gloved hand, resting on top of the passenger door. "Could you clear a path for me, do you think? And maybe help me call for assistance, since you speak the lingo?"

I looked inside the car again. "You haven't called for a tow truck?"

She shook her head. "I didn't know who to call."

I frowned. "And how long have you been sitting here?"

She glanced at the clock on the dashboard and seemed startled at what she saw. "Two hours," she said with a slight panic and a lot of annoyance. "I must have dozed off. Damn it."

I took a step back and beckoned to her to come over to the passenger side. "Come here. I will carry you through the nettles."

Her eyes widened and her cheeks turned a bright red. "Oh no," she said firmly. "That's *not* gonna happen." She gestured at the nettles. "Can't you just pull them out to make a path for me. You're wearing gloves."

I frowned. "No, I don't need that many."

It was clear from her face that she didn't understand. "Well, you won't be able to carry me," she said, looking me up and down. "No offense and all that, but you don't exactly look like the Hulk from where I'm sitting."

I wasn't sure what she meant by that. "Move over here," I said, gesturing to the passenger seat. "I will carry you."

She looked like she was going to protest again, but instead, she did as I had said. She had to lift her legs high to get across the mid console, and I was offered an even more generous vista of those glorious thighs before she slid into the passenger seat and pulled her skirt down. I leaned forward and slid one arm under her legs and the other around her back.

"I'm telling you right now, you're not going to be able to—" she said but stopped talking abruptly as I picked her up and started walking back toward the edge of the nettle patch.

I was grateful for the thick gloves, so that I didn't have to feel her warm skin with my bare hands. It was bad enough that I had her soft, round body pressing up against my chest, and her light and delicate scent invaded my nostrils with every breath. I pushed through the nettles over to the edge of the patch and put her down on the path I had made through the tall grass, coming here almost every day for the last couple of months. Then I quickly took a step back to get away from her alluring body. There was a part of me that hadn't wanted to let go of her, and I couldn't let that part get the upper hand. Never again. Oh no.

"I will lock the car," I said. "Is there anything in there that you need? The tow truck might be a while."

"My tote bag," she said, and I turned and waded back through the greenery, making sure to take the same way, so as not to crush any more of the delicious nettles than was absolutely necessary. Leaning inside the car to retrieve the tote bag and the key fob I heard her calling out behind me. "And my paints. They're in the backseat."

Glancing over the backrest, I spotted a large wooden box with a handle. I had to open the back door to get it out. When all the car doors were closed and locked, I made my way back to her. She reached for her things, but I only handed her the tote and the key fob. The wooden box was heavy, and it was a bit of a walk back. I retrieved my bucket of nettles from the fence post and gestured at her to walk ahead of me. The path wasn't wide enough for us to walk side by side.

Walking behind her didn't however offer me the relief that I had hoped for. Sure, I didn't have to see her beautiful face, but the sight of her round hips moving back and forth, causing the thin skirt to sway from side to side, was enough to make my chest constrict. And those round buttocks, clearly visible through the thin fabric with no panty line in sight. Wasn't she wearing any underwear? I tightened my grip on the heavy wooden box and forced myself to look away.

We reached the end of the path, at the edge of the field. A wooden door was partially hidden by the ivy that enveloped most of the stone wall that surrounded the property.

"Through here," I said, leaning past her to open the door. It was warped from age and often stuck against the door frame unless you gave it a hard tug.

Her eyes widened when the door flung open. She glanced at me, as if to try and decide if she should go with me. Then she peered inside suspiciously.

What she saw on the other side of the door made her suspiciousness vanish, though, and she gave off a small gasp. "Oh my…"

"Please, enter," I said. "I will call the garage. You can wait here until all the arrangements are made."

She stepped through the door, looking around her. "What is this place?" she said, breathlessly.

"This is the Monasterio de Camillo."

Her head spun round, and she stared at me. "A monastery? Are you a monk?"

It was probably intended as a joke, but I didn't smile. "It *used to be* a monastery," I said, walking past her toward the kitchen entrance. "Now it is an Agriturismo."

"What is that?" she asked, following me on the curved path through the well-kept garden. I didn't notice it anymore, but all the guests seemed very impressed by it. For me, it was just the place where I lived and worked.

"An Agriturismo … it's like a hotel in the countryside, where there are animals and the guests can experience the genuine Italian way of life," I said automatically. I had repeated those words more times than I cared to remember. Apparently, it was not a concept well known outside of Italy.

I opened the kitchen entrance and beckoned her inside. She walked past me without hesitation this time, and up the two small stone steps to the door, disappearing inside.

The kitchen felt dark after the intense sunshine outside, but my eyes soon adjusted, and I walked over to the large kitchen island in the middle of the room and put the bucket of nettles next to the sink. Then I continued through the spacious kitchen, over to my office. She lagged behind and I glanced at her. She was taking it all in with wide eyes, and I tried to picture what it must look like to her. It was a working kitchen with everything that a modern hotel needed, with plenty of sinks, gas burners, ovens, pots and pans and every utensil known to man arranged neatly above every workstation. It probably looked completely normal for someone coming in from outside, but if she had seen the rest of the building, she would have thought it stood out like a sore thumb, just like I did. But the authorities had their rules, and if I wanted to keep cooking for the guests here, I had to follow them.

Rummaging through the piles of correspondence on my desk, I unearthed my phone, and was relieved to see that there was still some power left in the battery. Scrolling through my contacts, I found the number of the local garage and pressed the little icon.

The phone rang, signal after signal, and I was just about to hang up when Giacomo picked up.

"Si?"

"Giacomo! It's Marco. There has been an accident. A car went off the road just east of here. Can you come and get it?"

There was no reply at first, and I became aware of the traffic noises in the background. Voices shouting and the roar of lorries going past. "Marco? Is that you?" Giacomo shouted. "I can barely hear you."

"Where are you?"

"There was a pile-up on the Autostrada. They've called in everyone in the district. I'll be here all afternoon." There was a pause. "And I've gotten three other calls while I've been here. I don't know when I can get to your car, I'm afraid. Is it off the road, completely? It's not blocking traffic?"

I turned around and leaned my bottom

against the desk. "No, it's far from the road. It's not blocking anything. It's in the middle of my nettle patch."

"Oh no!" I couldn't help but smile at the genuine despair in Giacomo's voice. "But … your soup?"

"Don't worry," I said reassuringly. "It's nearly the end of the season anyway."

Giacomo muttered something that got lost in the engine noise from another lorry. "I'll come round and get that car out of your nettles tomorrow," he promised.

"Great. And bring Lucia over for dinner one night when you're not working."

"I will!"

I ended the call and put the phone back down. When I returned to the kitchen, the woman was still standing where I had left her, looking interestedly at everything around her.

"I'm sorry," I said. "But there's been a pile-up on the Autostrada, and the man from the garage can't get here today."

A small frown appeared between her eyebrows. "Well, can't you call someone else?"

I shrugged. "There is no one else. Every tow truck in the district is busy."

"But … How do I get my car back on the road?"

"You don't. You will have to make other arrangements. Where were you headed?"

"Siena."

"Well, that's not far. I can call you a taxi. Or, if you have hotel reservations, they might be able to come and pick you up."

"No, I'm staying in Florence." She looked bewildered. "I was just going to Siena on a day trip, to paint. It's supposed to be so beautiful there." She glanced at the window that was mounted high on the wall. "But even if I could get there, I will have missed most of the daylight by now."

"I can find out when there's a train back to Firenze," I said. "And there might be someone here that can take you to the station." I gestured at her to follow. "Come with me."

READ the rest of Heather and Marco's story in Ravished.

www.ingramcontent.com/pod-product-compliance
Lightning Source LLC
Chambersburg PA
CBHW071617150726
48000CB00004B/1758